Liberty Awakened

by

Alicia Dean

Isle of Fangs Book 1

Liberty Awakened

Cover Art by *Lisa Dawn MacDonald*

The Wild Rose Press, Inc.
PO Box 708
Adams Basin, NY 14410-0708
Visit us at www.thewildrosepress.com

Publishing History
First Edition, 2022
Trade Paperback ISBN 978-1-5092-3978-8
Digital ISBN 978-1-5092-3979-5

Previously Self-published
Published in the United States of America

Liberty braced her hands on the door, intending to step back. Before she could, Eli lifted his head and whipped it toward her. He couldn't have heard her, could he? She'd barely made a sound. Maybe he just sensed—

Her thoughts ceased when she took a closer look at Eli's face. He stood in place, breathing heavily. She narrowed her eyes. God. No. His features were somehow distorted, his skin had a gray cast and looked…crumpled. His eyes glowed red. Something dark and liquid—blood?—was smeared around his mouth, dripped off his…fangs?

"No!" She let out the cry before she could stop herself, then clamped a hand over her mouth. Backing from the door, she shook her head violently from side to side. It couldn't be. No way. She had to have imagined it. A sound at the door told her Eli was coming out.

She turned and fled. Her tennis shoes slapped the ground, the noise reverberating in her ears along with the word—vampire…vampire…vampire. Oh my God. Vampire… Bats… Drained…

Acknowledgments

I would like to thank my Beta readers, Annie Delsignore Isabelle Gronlund, and Erin Sanders. The feedback from the three of you was priceless. And thank you to my fabulous critique partners, Kathy Wheeler and Christy Gronlund. You ladies keep me on my toes, and I could not do this without you. Thank you also to my brother, Brett Robertson, for his assistance with the bow training. I didn't have a clue how to use a bow, let alone how to teach my character to. I hope I got it right. And thank you to my sister, Christi, for helping to organize the Beta read and for always being a fan, and my niece, Madi, for her help with teen slang. Love you both so much.

Prologue

Sang Croc Island, French Polynesia

"No way am I going in there." Caitlin halted at the mouth of the cave, then planted her hands on her hips and turned to Ashton. "Not even for a fountain of youth."

She mentally crossed her fingers as she waited for his reply. If she didn't go, he would go without her. He would leave her out here alone. In the jungle.

The palm trees that were so pretty in the daytime now looked menacing. The sun had set and it was dark. Really dark. And she kept hearing strange noises. Some kind of animals… or murderers.

"It's not a fountain of youth." Even in the darkness, she could see Ashton roll his eyes. "It's a *stream*."

Caitlin bit her lip, trying to decide whether he was worth the risk. She loved him, and he was definitely hot--even hotter now than he had been before. Since they'd arrived on the island, his skin had tanned, and he'd become more muscular. He'd taken to going shirtless more often than not…and she certainly was *not* complaining.

"Whatever." She crossed her arms over her chest. "I doubt the *stream* of youth even exists."

"It exists. I know it. And when we find it, we'll be freakin' set for life." Ashton flipped his blond braids over his shoulder.

She'd hated the braids at first, but now she found them sexy. *Really* sexy…

She was weakening, but she tried once more. "There are, like, a million caves on this island. What makes you think this is the one?"

He grinned and gestured to the opening of the cave. "Only one way to find out."

Damn. He wasn't going to give up. She dropped her arms and let out a resigned breath, then followed him in.

Inside the cave, it was darker than it had been outside. Darker than anything she could have imagined. A musty odor tickled her nose, but she held back a sneeze. She didn't want to draw the attention of whatever creeped in the blackness.

"Turn on your flashlight," she whispered.

He did, but it wasn't much better. The beam played on the rocky, slime-covered walls of the cave. She shuddered.

He stopped abruptly, and she stumbled into him.

"Listen," he said. "Did you hear that?"

She concentrated. A rushing sound came to her ears. "Is it water?"

"Sounds like it." His voice rose with excitement. "Come on."

He took hold of her hand and pulled her along with him. She didn't have the heart to remind him that just because they found water, it wasn't necessarily *the* water.

With each moment that passed, the sound grew louder. Only now it didn't sound like water. It sounded like wings… flapping wings.

Oh shit.

Ashton must have seen the bat at the same time she

did. He dropped her hand and the flashlight. The beam played on his crouched figure, arms covering his head. She let out a scream, but his was louder.

God. He was a wuss. His screams grew more frantic. He was more afraid than she was. The creature flapped past her, brushing her arm. She ducked, her knees weak with terror, and slapped at the beast. She touched its creepy, hairy wing and another scream left her throat.

Whirling, she squinted in the nearly pitch black.

"Come on," she panted to Ashton. "Let's get the hell out of here before it comes back."

Ashton didn't rise. He rocked and muttered curses.

She grabbed his arm. She wouldn't leave him behind, even though she now found him considerably less attractive than he'd been moments ago.

"Get up. We have to go."

He finally stood, and she tugged, pulling him back the way they'd come.

The flapping sounded again. Her head whipped from side to side. The ginormous bat appeared directly in front of her. She screeched to a halt, shielding her face with her hands.

Ashton's girlish scream sent chills over her spine. Her heart pounded, but the nausea in her throat at his cowardice was more overwhelming.

"Jesus, grow some," she snapped. "We'll just take it slow and easy. I think the worst that could happen is… what? He bites us and we get rabies? Bats aren't all that vicious, right?"

She was talking more to herself than to Ashton. Or might as well be. He was a blubbering mess. No freakin' help at all.

The bat slowed, hovering in the air directly in front

of her. A noise like creaking leather and snapping twigs filled the cave. In disbelief, she watched his body stretch and grow, elongate.

Impossible.

The small head with the beady eyes morphed into… a man's face. Dear God. Terror seized her chest, and a whimper left her clogged throat.

"Jesus Christ," Ashton sobbed from behind her.

A man now stood where the bat had been moments before. His mouth drew into a grotesque smile. A black cape hung from his shoulders. He was over six feet tall with spiky blond hair that shimmered like flames in the meager glow of the flashlight. In his pale face, eyes the color of rubies blazed in the darkness.

"Oh my God," she choked out.

Ashton's blood curdling scream drowned out her words.

The creature glanced behind her toward Ashton. "You know, your boyfriend is a pussy." His oddly beautiful yet chilling eyes came back to her. "And just an FYI, this isn't the right cave." He smiled. "You're very cold."

"Wha—what are you?" The words pushed from her frozen vocal cords.

He threw his head back and laughed. His mouth opened, revealing long, sharp incisors.

No way… it couldn't be… a *vampire*?

With one hand, he grabbed her arm and jerked her off her feet and against his body. She caught a glimpse of a dagger tattoo along his jawline before his hand tangled in her hair and pulled her head back so far, she thought her neck would break.

"No, please," she sobbed. "Oh God, no.'" A sharp

4

sting pierced her neck. She struggled to pull away, but his grip and the suction of his mouth held her tightly to him.

A gray haze clouded her vision. Her body twitched, weakness flooding her limbs. A sucking sound filled her ears. Dimly, she was aware of Ashton passing in her peripheral. He was running, leaving her…

Without pausing in his tasting of her, the creature shot a hand out and snatched Ashton by the neck, lifting him off the ground. The snapping sound was the last thing she heard before she descended into blackness.

Chapter 1

Newcastle, Oklahoma

Liberty Delacort couldn't remember when she'd been happier. She'd graduated from high school tonight and was now secluded in an alcove with her boyfriend, Cam, a guy she'd loved since the moment she saw him in ninth grade. Even though she could hear their friends laughing, could hear Florence and the Machine's "Never Let Me Go," the sounds seemed miles away from hers and Cam's private oasis amidst the after-graduation party.

Cam slipped an arm around her waist and kissed her. His lips were warm, nice. His hand moved up her back and pressed her against his body. His other hand crept upward. For the first time ever, he slipped his hand inside her shirt and touched her bare breast.

She drew in a breath and grabbed his wrist. "Don't."

"Come on, babe." Cam's sandy brown hair flopped on his forehead, covering one of his gorgeous blue eyes. "I've waited a long time. You can't keep doing this to me."

Liberty bit her lip, torn between wanting to please him and knowing she wasn't ready. "I-I can't. I'm sorry. We said we'd wait."

"We have waited." A hard edge tinged the words. "But we graduated tonight. We're adults now. We've been together four years. What's the big deal?"

"I'm just not ready."

His mouth turned down in a bitter frown. "I'm starting to wonder if you'll ever be ready."

Misery weighted her chest. "Me too."

He grunted and shook his head. "I don't get it. What are you waiting for?"

"I don't know."

But she did know. She'd read a romance novel once where the heroine said the hero's touch made the blood rush to her head. Made her weak with desire. She couldn't think straight when he touched her. Everything inside her cried out for him to make love to her. That was what Liberty wanted. And in spite of how much she loved Cam, nothing remotely like that happened when he kissed her, when he touched her. If she ever experienced that kind of passion, then she'd be ready. Yeah, sure, it was fiction. And she might die a virgin, but she wasn't willing to give up on that dream. Not yet.

Cam ran a hand through his hair. He opened his mouth, but before he spoke, a loud crash like breaking glass sounded, followed by a male scream and female shrieks.

"What the hell?" Cam bit out.

He brushed past her, hurrying into the living room. Liberty followed.

Del Collona lay in a bed of broken beer bottles, writhing and screaming. Half a dozen people stood around him, mouths gaping open. The rest of the crowd seemed oblivious to the accident and continued partying.

Blood seeped from beneath Del's body. Liberty froze, covering her mouth with her hand to hold in a scream. Nausea cramped her stomach. Her legs went weak, and black spots danced before her eyes.

"For God's sake, someone call 9-1-1." Cam squatted beside Del, gently rolling him to inspect his injuries.

Liberty couldn't move. Her cell was in her pocket, but she couldn't make her hands work.

Blood. She shuddered. The sight of blood terrified her, made her want to vomit, but she couldn't seem to look away.

Voices rose around her.

What happened?

Marcus dared him to dive into those beer bottles.

And he did it? What a dufus.

"Are you okay?" Her best friend, Alyssa, took her arm and gave it a shake. "Liberty, are you all right?"

Liberty nodded. "We need to—to call…"

"I called 9-1-1. They're on their way."

"Okay. Good." Liberty found the willpower to turn away. She clutched her stomach and doubled over, gritting her teeth against the nausea. *I will not throw up. I will not throw up…*

Alyssa rubbed her back. "It's okay. He'll be fine."

How did she know? He might *not* be fine. He could die.

In moments, the sound of sirens penetrated her numbness. The front door flew open, and two EMT's entered, wheeling a gurney between them. Liberty didn't turn around, didn't want to watch as they treated Del… as they wheeled him past her and out the door.

"I'm going to the hospital." She dug her keys out of her jeans pocket.

"Are you sure?" Alyssa's concerned features swam in her vision. They'd been friends since the first grade. Alyssa knew about her blood phobia. "I'll come with you."

Liberty looked around Cam's living room. His parents were out of town, and he'd thrown the party without their permission. He'd be toast.

"No. Why don't you stay and help Cam clean up. His parents will be back tomorrow."

"If you're sure."

"Yeah, I am. I'll be fine."

Cam appeared behind Alyssa and looked over her shoulder at Liberty. "You're leaving?"

"I'm going to check on Del. I should probably call his mom."

Cam took hold of her hand and squeezed. "Are you coming back?"

"No. It might be late by the time I'm done at the hospital. We'll talk tomorrow, okay? I'll call once I know how Del is."

"Sure. Okay." He kissed her on the cheek and released her. His eyes showed his disappointment.

Alyssa took her into a tight hug. "Sorry this night turned out so sucky. But hey, graduation. Pretty cool, am I right?"

Liberty forced a smile. "Right. Done with high school. We'll be college roomies in the fall."

"Can't wait." Alyssa returned the smile and hugged her again.

Cam walked her to her car. The neighborhood was still, quiet. A cool spring breeze wafted over her, and she shivered. Before she slid inside her Cobalt, he said, "Are you sure you don't want to come back? Finish our conversation?"

"I'm sure. It's been a crazy night." She was frightened for Del and had no idea how long she'd be at the hospital. All the fun had been sucked out of the evening, and she was sure she'd be ready to crash by the time the long night ended. Besides, she didn't want to continue their conversation. Didn't want more pressure from Cam. Not ready meant *not ready*.

Cam's mouth tightened, but he didn't say more. He stepped back and let her drive away.

The hour she spent at the hospital seemed like ten. Del's mom showed up, hysterical and accusatory, demanding that Liberty explain what happened. Liberty was tempted to tell her the truth. That her idiot, drunken son had dive-bombed into a stack of beer bottles. Instead, she told her she had no idea, and that she should talk to Del, who, as it turned out, would be fine. A dozen stitches and some pain killers, and they released him into his distraught and furious mother's care. Liberty texted Alyssa and Cam with the good news.

Once in the car, Liberty's exhaustion fled. She was hyped, antsy. Cam was probably still up. She needed to see him. Feel his arms around her. Maybe even…

Should she? She loved Cam, and he loved her. Maybe that was enough. Yes. It was enough. They'd been together four years. They would be together forever. It was time.

Her heart lifted as she headed to Cam's house. She'd made her decision, and it felt right. Cam would be surprised, and thrilled.

When she pulled up to the curb, the lights were off, and all the cars were gone. Except Alyssa's Acura. Was she still helping him clean? If so, why were the lights off?

A niggle of dread tugged at Liberty's heart. She didn't acknowledge what the dread represented. There could be a perfectly logical explanation for her best friend to still be at her boyfriend's house. *With the lights off...*

Not bothering to knock on the front door, she tried the knob. Unlocked. Either they were doing something perfectly innocent, or they weren't all that bright.

Cam came down the stairs the moment she stepped into the foyer. He flipped a switch, and light bathed the room. He wore nothing but jeans, unbuttoned, the flaps gaping open. His face paled.

"Hey, Liberty. I thought you weren't coming back." His voice was uneven. He sounded like a bad actor in a doomed audition.

"What's going on?" Liberty demanded.

"What do you mean?" He stretched his arms above his head and yawned, then rubbed a hand over his face. "I was asleep."

She gave a humorless laugh. "Are you really that dumb? Or do you just think I am? Alyssa's car is outside. Where is she?"

His mouth opened and closed like a fish gasping for air, but no words came out.

She stormed toward him and headed up the stairs. "Alyssa!"

He tried to grab her arm, but she evaded his touch.

Liberty threw Cam's door open and halted just inside his room. Although she'd known the truth, seeing it first hand, confirming it, made her heart clench with pain.

Alyssa stood by the bed. She'd managed to dress, but the last few buttons of her shirt were undone, and she was searching frantically on the floor. Looking for her shoes? Her blonde hair had that mussed, just crawled out of bed look. Because she had. Just crawled out of bed.

Liberty had always been envious of Alyssa's perfect hair. Her own brown hair never looked as good as Alyssa's. Even now, with it sticking up in places, her hair was gorgeous. Liberty shook her head. Now was not the time to admire the traitor's hair.

"How could you do this?" Sobs choked Liberty's voice. She hadn't even realized she was crying, but now she felt the dampness on her cheeks.

Alyssa's eyes filled with tears too, and she gave up her search. "I'm so, so sorry. Oh my God. I'm sorry."

Liberty drew in a shaky breath and shook her head. "You're the last person I thought would betray me."

Liberty wasn't aware Cam had entered the room until he spoke behind her. "Listen, babe. I know you're upset, but come on, you weren't giving it up. This didn't mean anything."

She whirled on him. "You, I'm not surprised." She turned back to Alyssa. "But you? I never would have believed you'd do something like this. Losing you hurts a lot worse."

Alyssa took a step toward her, hand outstretched. "Then don't… don't lose me. We can get past this."

Liberty lifted her chin and swiped at her tears. "Maybe you can. But I can't."

****

The next day, Liberty lay in bed, hating herself for being such a Gloomy Glenda, but unable to summon the energy to do anything other than mope.

Alyssa and Cam had called and texted so many times, she'd finally grown tired of ignoring them and shut off her phone. They'd actually had the nerve to come by her house—separately—but she'd told her mother to send them away. Fortunately, being a Saturday, the doctor's office where her mother worked as a nurse was closed. Liberty was grateful to have a buffer between her and the asshole and his skank.

Her mother had asked what was wrong, but Liberty didn't tell her. Most likely, she'd put two and two together, but she was giving Liberty her space. That was one of the things she loved most about her mom. She knew when to reach out and when to back off. It had just been the two of them all these years. Her real father had died when she was a baby, and her mother had never remarried. They were more like girlfriends than mother and daughter. And after losing Alyssa, Liberty definitely needed a friend. She just wasn't ready to talk about it yet.

"Sweetheart?" Her mother's muffled voice carried from the other side of the closed door.

"Mom, I'm sorry. I just want to be alone."

"You got something in the mail."

Liberty considered ignoring her, then with a sigh, she threw back the covers and climbed from bed. When she opened the door, her mother smiled worriedly and handed her an envelope.

Liberty took the package. "Thanks, Mom."

Danielle Delacort nodded, her concerned gaze searching Liberty's face. She was thirty-six—still young—yet she'd barely ever dated. Liberty never understood that. Men were definitely interested in her. She was attractive—a MILF—as Liberty's crude guy friends called her. Liberty looked nothing like her blonde-haired, brown-eyed mother. She always figured she'd taken after her father with her darker hair and green eyes. But she'd never seen a picture of him. Her mother didn't have one. Their relationship had been short-lived, he'd died young, and that was that. No memories, no photos, no nothing. As if he'd only existed for the purpose of creating Liberty, then poof, he was gone.

"Are you hungry?" her mom asked. "I could make you something, or we could go grab a bite."

"I'm not, but thanks. Maybe later."

She gently cupped Liberty's cheek. "I'm here for you, sweetie."

"I know." Liberty made herself smile, although it strained her jaw to do so.

Liberty closed the door behind her mother and plopped back on the bed to check out the envelope. The return address was Sang Croc, French Polynesia. What the freak? It must be a mistake. She didn't know anyone who lived anywhere near the French Polynesian Islands. She tore open the flap and reached inside, pulling out a folded sheet of paper and a stack of photos.

The first photo showed a small girl—maybe two or three years old—resting on the hip of a tall, dark-haired man. They stood on a white sand beach next to a palm tree. In the background was an endless expanse of the bluest water she'd ever seen. She peered more closely at the child in the picture, and her heart thumped heavily, painfully in her chest.

The child was her.

But how? She'd never been to an island in her life. Had she? Maybe she and her mom had taken a trip there when she was little. But surely her mom would have mentioned it. Would have had photos from their trip. And who was this man? She thumbed through the remaining pictures. A knot settled in the pit of her stomach. Some of the shots were of Liberty, the man… and her mother.

She unfolded the letter and read.

Dear Liberty,

I know this will come as a shock, but the time has arrived that you must know the truth. You have been told that your father died when you were a baby. That is not true. He is alive, but now, alas, just barely. His name is Victor Van Helsing. He is quite ill, and I am afraid he has little time left. He does not know I am writing to you, but it is urgent that you come to the island immediately. You are desperately needed for many reasons.

The enclosed photographs are proof that I speak the truth. I am certain you find the news confusing, disconcerting, and difficult to believe, but please know, it is *the truth. More than that, it is your destiny.*

Enclosed you will find a round trip ticket to Tahiti, where you will take a boat for the rest of your journey to Sang Croc, and a US certified check for your travel funds. The round trip ticket is for your peace of mind. You may return home at any time. Please understand that I am trusting you to do the right thing. It has not escaped my attention that you can cash the check and never contact me. Knowing your father's blood runs in your veins, I do not believe that will be the course of action you choose. I feel strongly that you will heed the call. Your destiny awaits.

Sincerely,

Antoine Favreau

Manservant to Victor Van Helsing

All feeling drained from Liberty's arms and legs. Impossible. Her mother wouldn't have lied to her. No way. This was some kind of mistake. She had to believe that. After what Alyssa and Cam had done to her, she couldn't handle learning her mother was just as devious.

But the photos… irrefutable proof. They weren't photo-shopped. They were genuine. She had been to this island. With her mother. And with this mysterious man—her father?

She sprang from the bed and threw open her bedroom door. "Mom!" Running down the stairs, she continued to call out, "Mom! Where are you?"

"For Pete's sake, Liberty. What's the matter?" Her mother came from the kitchen, drying her hands on a dish towel.

"This." Liberty thrust the letter and photos toward her mother.

Danielle took them, her brows drawn into a puzzled frown. The frown deepened as she read and flipped through the photos. When she looked up, her face was pale, her mouth drawn, confusion evident in her eyes. Liberty had expected guilt, fear, shame, and deception. Not such deep bewilderment.

"What is this? Who sent it? Is it some kind of joke?"

"You tell me, Mother. Apparently, Mr. Antoine Favreau, who works for my father, sent it. You know, my father who is supposedly dead!"

She slowly shook her head. "He is dead. He died when you were a baby. I have no idea who this man is."

Liberty tapped the photo of her mother. "You know who that is, right? It's you."

Danielle squinted at the photo. "It looks like me. That's definitely you. But I don't know this man. I've never been to this island—to any island. It's some kind of hoax."

"Unbelievable." Liberty snatched the stack from her mother's hands. She swallowed back tears. She'd done enough crying in the past twelve hours. It was now time for action. "I don't know why you lied to me all these years, why you're still lying when the proof is staring you in the face, but when I get to Sang Croc, I'll get my answers."

Her mother's face drained of color. "What? You surely don't plan to go. That's insane. We have no idea who these people are or what they want. It could be some kind of sex slave ring."

Liberty laughed. "A sex slave ring that has photos of me and my mother? That sends me a round trip plane ticket to an exotic, tropical island and two-thousand dollars? If that's the case, it's the *ultimate* sex slave ring, wouldn't you say?"

"Don't be a smartass." Her mother's mouth tightened. "You can't seriously think I'm going to allow you to go."

Liberty snorted. "You can't seriously think you can stop me. I'm eighteen years old. I caught my boyfriend and my best friend in bed together last night. *On* graduation night."

"You what? Oh, honey—"

Liberty cut her off. "I just found out you've lied to me all these years about my father. You told me he was *dead*. I get an opportunity for the trip of my life, and to find out answers to questions I didn't even know I had. You really think I'm going to let you stop me?"

Tears spilled down her mom's cheeks. "You can't— can't leave me." She looked defeated, older somehow.

"You shouldn't have lied."

"I swear, sweetheart. I don't know what's going on, but I did *not* lie." She covered her mouth with her hand. A small sob escaped. "I would never do that to you. You're my world."

Guilt and sympathy tamped down Liberty's anger. Her mother looked so lost… so broken and wounded. Much like Liberty felt.

Still gripping the photos and documents in her hand, Liberty put her arms around her and hugged. Her mother squeezed back, holding tightly as if afraid to let go.

Liberty's conscience waffled between hurt at her mother's apparent betrayal, and fear of leaving her home. Could she really do this? Take off for a faraway place with strangers she'd never met? With a father she'd never known was alive?

Chapter 2

Liberty sat next to her mother in the airport. For the past week, they'd argued off and on, cried, and given one another the silent treatment. Nothing had really been resolved, other than Liberty had decided she had to go.

"Are you sure? I wish I could convince you I'm not lying. These people are phonies." Her mother's teary voice was starting to wear on Liberty. At times, it made her feel guilty. Others, just annoyed.

Liberty took her hand. "Mom, I love you more than anything. I know you only lied to protect me. That you're still not telling me the truth, because you don't want me to go."

Danielle shook her head. "I'm so afraid for you, but I swear, I'm telling the truth."

Liberty gritted her teeth and hissed out a breath. "Please. My flight leaves soon. Let's not spend these last minutes going over the same thing we've been over a hundred times."

Her mother nodded, tears hovering in her brown eyes.

Bottom line, nothing could stop Liberty from traveling to this mysterious, captivating place. Three of the people she trusted most had betrayed her—even though she was aware her mother did it for what she thought was best for Liberty. She couldn't breathe in her home town any longer. Besides… *your destiny awaits…*

How could she resist a line like that?

****

Liberty was so blown away by the beauty of the island, she didn't even care that much that she was homesick and terrified to meet this stranger who was supposedly her father.

She pressed her face to the taxi window so she wouldn't miss a thing. The water of the South Pacific was a crystal clear blue-green. She could actually make out movement of fish below the surface when the taxi slowed to take a sharp turn. Tall slender palm trees bordered the road, stretching like ballerinas toward the vivid blue of the sky. It was late afternoon, and the sun shimmered like molten gold.

She lifted the garland of pink-tipped petals to her nose, inhaling the fragrant scent of the plumeria lei a pretty Polynesian girl had placed around her neck when she stepped off the plane. She hadn't been here an hour and was already receiving the entire island experience. She would feel as though she'd landed in paradise if her reasons for coming were a little less troubling.

Her mouth dropped open when they passed a row of huts suspended above the ocean on stilts. "What are those?" she blurted.

"They're bungalows. The owners rent them out, mostly to tourists. Tourists eat that shit up."

She'd almost forgotten about the cab driver—he'd introduced himself as Ryan Kelly—until he answered her. He was a few years older than she was and had dark hair and sort of squinty brown eyes that looked like he was smiling, even when he wasn't. He was Australian—or at least that's what his accent sounded like. He was pretty hot—she'd noticed him even before he offered her a ride. But once the scenery captivated her attention, even a sexy Australian guy faded into oblivion.

"I bet they do. That's awesome." She craned her neck so she could keep looking at the bungalows until they were no longer in sight.

"So how long are you here for?" Ryan asked.

"I'm not sure. Probably a while."

"Are you a friend of Victor Van Helsing?"

He was looking at her intently in the rear view mirror. All she could see was his eyes, so she wasn't sure if he was smiling, but he was definitely being nosy.

She considered how to answer, then settled on, "My parents knew him."

There. Vague and *somewhat* honest. She wasn't about to share her life history with a stranger in a strange new place. Of course, everyone here was a stranger to her. Even her father.

"Well, I hope you enjoy your stay, however long it may be."

"I googled the island before I came. I read that a large number of people are killed or go missing from here. Is that true?"

He shrugged and glanced at her in the mirror again. "Not really. Just rumors that circulate because so many people who visit our island decide to stay. They never go back home."

"But wouldn't their families know that? They wouldn't be missing then. And it seems to me the island would become overpopulated very quickly."

Another shrug. "You know how rumors go. Urban legends and the like."

His explanation was less than satisfactory. Too vague. Something in his tone made her feel he wasn't being completely honest. *I guess that makes two of us.*

"I also read that tourists keep coming because of a cave with water that prevents aging?" Even as she said the words, she didn't believe them, but she was fascinated with what she'd learned in her computer search. Given how he had hedged around her previous question, she was curious about how he would handle this one.

"It doesn't exist, but yes, it keeps tourists coming. That and the beauty of the island. Not to mention, it's a reasonably priced getaway. We offer extremely low rates on accommodations, food, entertainment."

"Why? Because if you didn't, people might not come since it's so dangerous?"

He laughed, but it sounded forced. His caginess was unsettling. What had she gotten herself into?

All conversation ceased when the taxi coasted up a winding drive to a massive three-story house.

"This is it," Ryan said.

"Wow," she breathed. Her gaze traveled over the stone façade, tall white pillars, wraparound porch, and large bay windows. "This is it, huh?"

"Yep. It's the largest house on the island. You'll be put up in style." He climbed out and opened her door. "I'll help you with your bags."

He reached for her hand, and everything inside her locked. What was she doing here? Fear pumped through her blood. She didn't know these people. She was worlds away from everything familiar. *I can't do this. Oh God, I can't do this.* She squeezed her eyes shut, fighting the terror.

"Hey, are you okay?"

She opened her eyes and stared up at Ryan. His

brows were drawn in a frown.

"I—I just…" She shuddered. She couldn't turn back now, right? "I'm a bit nervous. I've actually never met… Mr. Van Helsing."

He reached into his pocket. "Here." He held out a large silver coin, and she took it.

She'd never seen a coin like it. One side held a crown, a flag, and the number fifty with the words, *Royal Visit 2000*. The other side was a headshot of Queen Elizabeth.

She looked up at Ryan. "What's this for?"

"When I was a small child, and I was worried about something or afraid, my father would tell me to wrap my fingers around the coin and feel its warmth. That would remind me that I'm real, grounded. The warmth proves that you're a living, breathing being. That alone gives you power."

Tears pricked the backs of her eyes. This gesture from a complete stranger made her feel a little less alone. She blinked to keep from crying and stretched her hand out toward him. "I can't take this. Your father gave it to you."

"It's not the same coin. That's just one I had on me." He closed his hand around hers. The coin and her skin warmed to his touch. "Please keep it. I insist."

She nodded and pulled back. A shaky breath left her body. He had definitely distracted her from her fear. He was *really* hot. Maybe too hot.

Smiling, she climbed from the car and looked at the house again. She'd never seen a house like this, other than on television or in magazines of celebrity homes.

She tugged her overnight bag onto her shoulder and squeezed her fist around the coin.

"You ready?" Ryan's chocolate brown eyes smiled into hers.

"Ready," she whispered. "Thank you."

He winked, then grabbed a suitcase in each hand and headed up the walk to the porch.

Before they could knock, the door swung open.

A Polynesian man with streaks of gray in his dark hair and skin the color of caramel smiled and stuck out his hand. "You must be Liberty. I am Antoine Favreau. Please, come in."

His voice was smooth with the hint of a French accent. Did everyone on the island have an accent? She stepped past him into the foyer, and Ryan followed.

"Ryan, thank you for bringing her."

"No problem." He looked from her to Antoine, curiosity evident in his eyes. "Would you like me to take her bags up?"

If he was waiting for enlightenment of who she was and why she was here, he was disappointed.

"No, thank you. That will be all." Antoine handed him some cash, then held the door open, an obvious hint.

Ryan turned to her. "Nice meeting you, Liberty. Hope to see you around. If you want a tour of the island, give me a shout."

"I will. Thanks." She almost blurted out for him not to leave her. Her stomach was knotted with apprehension. The elegant interior matched the outside of the house, making her feel ghetto in comparison. Not to mention, she was about to meet her long lost father. She had an urge to flee, but she gripped the coin in her fist and forced herself to stay.

After Ryan left, Antoine gestured toward a doorway. "Please, come in and sit. Your father is resting. We can talk for a moment before I take you up to meet him."

She slipped the coin inside a pocket of her overnight bag, then followed him into a large room—were there any other kind in this house?—and settled into a lush, tan suede sofa, placing her bag on the floor next to her.

"Would you like a drink? Sherry, wine?"

"I'm only eighteen."

He smiled, showing white teeth in his brown skin. "I assure you I am not breaking any laws. The drinking age here is eighteen."

She rubbed damp palms on the thighs of her jeans and shook her head. "I'm not much of a drinker."

"Very well then. Soda?"

"No, thank you. I'm good."

He went behind a bar that stretched along one wall of the room and poured red liquid from a decanter into a glass, then sat on a chair adjacent to the sofa.

"This must be a bit unsettling for you."

"Yes, it's pretty insane. I mean, I've been told my entire life my father died. Now, you tell me he's alive. My mother swore she hadn't lied to me. That she'd never been to this island, but I saw the pictures…"

She still couldn't wrap her mind around the fact that her mother would blatantly lie, even when confronted with the evidence. How could she do that?

Something secretive flashed in Antoine's expression, then was quickly masked. "She likely felt it in your best interest to keep the truth from you. Your father wanted to protect you, so he agreed to let you go."

"Protect me from what?"

He frowned into his glass before bringing it to his lips and taking a sip. "You will learn the entire truth in time. For now, suffice it to say that the situation surrounding your father—and you—is quite extraordinary."

"Extraordinary how?"

"I am afraid I cannot tell you everything right now. I promised Mr. Van Helsing that I would not."

"You brought me here to meet my father, and you won't even tell me what's going on?" Her voice rose, even though she'd intended to stay calm. Half of her wanted to hear the entire truth, and that part was frustrated by the secrecy. The other half wished she'd destroyed the letter and forgotten she'd ever received it. But that course of action would have had its own problems—like dealing with a traitorous boyfriend and wayward best friend.

"I promised him I would not tell you as long as he is alive. But once he is gone…" In spite of his professionalism and formality, his voice was raspy with emotion, his mouth drawn in sadness. He was apparently pretty close to Victor. How hard would that be to watch someone you care about die, right before your eyes?

A shudder ran through her. "Is it really that bad?"

"I would not have called you if it were not."

"What's wrong with him?" She didn't even know what he was dying from.

Again, a secretive look crossed his face, and he was silent for several moments. Finally, he said, "He was injured. I cannot go into details now, but the injuries were too severe to recover from. Now, it is only a matter of time. A very short time according to physicians."

She drew in a deep breath and let it out slowly. "I think I'll take that drink now."

"White wine? Or maybe red? What is your preference?"

"White is fine."

He stood, going to the bar and pouring from a bottle he retrieved from a small stainless steel refrigerator. He brought her the glass, and she gulped half the contents. She drank so fast, she barely had a chance to appreciate the crisp, fruity flavor. The alcohol gave her a nice tingle in her belly, relaxing her.

"Shall we go up and see your father?"

She swallowed the rest of the wine and nodded. When she rose, her head swam with dizziness. She hadn't lied. She wasn't much of a drinker, and the wine combined with nervousness made her afraid she might pass out.

She drew in a steadying breath and followed Antoine up a winding staircase, the ascent increasing her dizziness. He halted in front of a door and eased it back. He went in first and motioned for her to follow. She stepped inside, her gaze going to the large four-poster bed. The figure of a man lay beneath the bronze-colored comforter, his head resting on a white pillow, eyes closed. They approached and he stirred, squinting up at Antoine.

"She is here, sir."

Victor lifted his head to stare past Antoine, directly at Liberty. Although his skin was sallow, his eyes rimmed with dark circles, remnants of the tall handsome man in the photos remained. His hair was a few shades lighter than her dark brown, and streaked with gray. His eyes were the same deep green as hers. She knew in that moment, this man was her father.

He scowled and glared at her for several seconds. Then his features softened. "Liberty?"

She'd never seen anyone near death, but the pallor

27

on his face and the weakness in his voice convinced her he was ill… deathly ill.

She nodded.

He looked at Antoine. "You shouldn't have brought her here."

"Yes, sir I knew it was against your wishes. But she needs to be here. She needs to know."

Know what? She wanted to scream, but the unsettling bleakness of the room kept her silent.

"You should leave the island," Victor said, his head dropping back to the pillow, his eyes drifting shut.

Tears rose to her throat, but she swallowed them back, wishing she'd kept hold of the coin. Her father had abandoned her years ago, and even now, at deaths door, he didn't want her. Too bad. She hadn't come this far to be sent away.

"I'm staying." Her voice was more confident than she expected, braver than she felt. As if her feet had grown roots, she remained planted in place.

He spoke again without opening his eyes. The words were barely above a whisper, but she heard them loud and clear. "Then God have mercy on your soul."

****

Liberty slept fitfully, even though the room Antoine showed her to couldn't have been more luxurious, the bed the most comfortable she'd ever been in. She woke early, showered and dressed, then went downstairs.

Antoine was in the kitchen. He'd prepared a breakfast of fluffy eggs, croissants, thinly sliced ham, and various tropical fruits—papaya, oranges, pineapple, and a few she couldn't identify. More food than she could possibly eat, even if she'd been hungry, which she wasn't. The knot from yesterday was still lodged in the pit of her stomach. She ate a few bites and thanked him before pushing the plate away.

"What are your plans for the day?" He took her plate, frowning down at it, but didn't say anything about how much food she'd left. "Would you like to take Ryan up on his offer to show you the island?"

"I would rather stick around. Maybe get to know Victor a little. I know he doesn't want me here, but I came to get to know him, right?"

"That is correct. However, I feel you should give him time to get used to your being here. Perhaps a day of relaxation and fun will prepare you for the weeks ahead."

Prepare for the weeks ahead? That sounded pretty ominous. Truthfully, she wasn't looking forward to another face to face with Victor just yet. A girl could only take so much rejection. "I suppose I could do a little sight-seeing. Maybe I could find some kind of job for however long I'm here."

"You will not need to work. Mr. Van Helsing will see to your needs and provide an allowance."

"Thanks, but I need to stay busy. Besides, I don't want to bum off of him. I'd rather make my own way."

"Very well, then. Ryan can assist you with the job search."

"I suppose. Do you know him well?"

"I do. He is a fine young man. Quite trustworthy. I can ring him if you like."

Ring him. So formal. "Sure. Yeah. Ring him."

He did, and Ryan agreed to come pick her up. She was looking forward to hanging out with him. He was the only other person she'd met on the island, and she couldn't stay inside this humongous house all day with a father who wanted her gone. Besides, she had thought about him a lot since yesterday. She couldn't deny there was something there. He seemed to like her too. Or maybe he looked at all the girls with that glimmer in his deep brown eyes, made them all feel like they were the only thing that mattered. Gave them all a fifty cent coin to help ground them…

An hour later, she and Ryan were driving along the same roads they'd traveled the evening before. This time, in a compact car instead of a taxi.

"What would you like to do?" He shot a glance at her from beneath a navy blue beanie that made him look boyish, cute.

"I'm not sure. What is there to do here?"

He flashed dimples. "What *isn't* there to do? We have gorgeous beaches, snorkeling, swimming with sharks, hang gliding—"

"Sharks and hang gliding?" She gaped at him. "How about something that won't kill me?"

He laughed. "I promise, you're perfectly safe with me."

He took hold of her hand where it rested on her lap and gave it a squeeze. A warm tingle raced up her arm. He really was fine. But she didn't need to crush on the first guy she met. Or any guy for that matter, not after the crap with Cam. Ryan took his hand away, and she breathed more freely.

"I'd actually like to find a job. Do you know of anyone who's hiring?"

"A job? You do plan to be here a while."

He was fishing for an explanation. He wouldn't get one. Antoine had insisted she not tell anyone that Victor was her father. She was happy to agree. It wasn't something she was ready to deal with, let alone talk about to anyone else.

"I don't know how long yet, but I might as well find something to do with my time."

"I think I know just the place. I work at a tiki bar. We're always looking for an extra set of hands. You interested?"

"I thought you were a cab driver."

"I do a little of everything. I can put in a word for you if you'd like. We could go there now."

Working at a tiki bar on an exotic island? And she thought she'd spend her summer behind a drive-thru window at a smelly fast food place. "Sure. That would be great."

The tiki bar sat on the beach. It was called The Perfect Getaway according to the wooden sign hanging above the door. The patio was furnished with bamboo chairs and tables that overlooked the water. As far as Liberty could tell, all of the tables were occupied. Torches flanked the entrance of what looked like a grass hut.

She and Ryan walked across a wooden plank and into the open doorway.

Just like the patio, bamboo tables and chairs were filled to capacity, as were the stools at the long bamboo bar. Liberty was surprised to hear contemporary music—"This Love" by Maroon 5—playing. She figured a place like this would play nothing but island music. The song made her wistful and helped her feel closer to home at the same time.

A tall, gorgeous girl with a perfect tan and midnight black curly hair who stood next to a nearby table spotted them and smiled. "Ryan, who's your friend?" Like Ryan, she had an Australian accent. His sister? Girlfriend? She wore a colorful blouse and a short skirt, which Liberty realized by glancing around must be a uniform.

"This is Liberty Delacort. Liberty, my sister, Bianca."

Why did she feel a slight sense of relief that the girl was his sister?

"Nice to meet you, Liberty. I'd shake hands but, well…" Bianca gestured with her head to the full tray of drinks she held. "Sorry, can't chat. We're slammed. You should get your bum to work, Ryan. Help us out, for cripes sake."

Before Ryan could respond, she was off serving the colorful drinks to a table in the corner.

"See?" Ryan smiled. "Told you we needed help."

Within a half hour, he'd introduced Liberty to his cranky American boss, Jerome—who hired her on the spot—found a uniform for her, and penciled her name in on the schedule.

"Bianca will train you, starting tomorrow." Ryan's wide grin made his eyes crinkle even more than usual. "Welcome aboard, Liberty."

She smiled back, but inside, her heart was beating so hard, her insides quaked. This suddenly felt real… and frighteningly permanent.

Chapter 3

Liberty didn't know if she was all that good at catching on, if Bianca was that good at teaching, or if the tiki bar was really that desperate for servers, but she was on her own after one evening of training.

On her second night of work, her first table was a couple in their mid-sixties, Nelda and Lester Rankin, and their thirteen-year-old granddaughter, Hannah.

She'd learned they were from Miami, Oklahoma—two-hundred miles from her home town, but close enough that it made her homesick.

"You're doing an exceptional job, dear," Nelda said when Liberty brought their drinks. "We're having the time of our lives here, and meeting a friendly face from home is icing on the cake."

"Thank you. I'm happy to meet people from home, too." Liberty was tempted to ask her for a hug, but refrained. She missed her mom... bad.

"I like your necklace." Hannah smiled shyly. She was thin and blonde, with braces she tried to cover up by smiling with her mouth closed and hiding behind her hand when she spoke. She had an awkward, subtle prettiness that would soon bloom into true beauty.

Liberty removed the friendship necklace Alyssa had given her when they were thirteen. It was a red and black jagged half heart with Liberty's name engraved on the back. Alyssa kept the other half. Liberty wasn't quite sure why she still wore it. It was as meaningless as their friendship had become.

"Thank you. Would you like to wear it?"

"Could I?"

"Sure." Liberty slid it over the girl's head. "You all will just have to make sure you come back before you leave so you can return it to me."

"Oh, we'll be back often," Nelda said. "We're here for the entire summer, and this is the best place we've found to eat."

Liberty smiled and headed to the kitchen to turn in their order.

Jerome blocked the doorway, his beefy face scarlet, his brows scrunched in anger. "You can't hang out at a table for that long and ignore your other customers. What the hell's wrong with you?"

She flinched, her face heating with embarrassment. A quick glance around told her there was an audience of a few co-workers, and at least one table of customers. Her first job ever, and she was getting reamed by the manager within the first week. "I'm sorry. I was just trying to be friendly."

"Try a little harder to be a *waitress*, why don't you. That's what I pay you for. You're on probation as of now. One more screw up, and you're gone."

"Back off her, Jerome."

Liberty turned at the sound of the voice. A guy who stood three or four inches taller than Jerome's 5'6, with shaggy dark blond hair and silver eyes glared at the manager. Liberty cringed, expecting Jerome to let loose on him as she'd seen him do to more than a few employees in the short time she'd been here.

Her mouth dropped open in shock when Jerome

bobbed his head emphatically. Where just a few seconds ago, he'd been furious, now fear shadowed his eyes.

"Eli." Jerome's voice was little more than a squeak. "Yeah, sure. Sorry." He looked at Liberty. "Sorry, Liberty. I shouldn't have lost my temper with you. You're new." The words were sincere, but she detected an underlying resentment. No wonder. He'd been as humiliated as she was just a few moments ago. Who was this newcomer who had Jerome shaking like a leaf in a tornado?

"Thank you." Liberty faced the stranger. "You didn't have to do that, though."

"I don't like bullies." He grinned. "And I don't like to see a pretty girl about to cry."

"I wasn't about to cry."

"Were too." His voice lowered, his eyes seeming to almost her as they roamed over her face, then down her body. She struggled to draw a full breath.

She spoke quietly. "You know, as nice as that was, I have to work here every day. Maybe you shouldn't have said anything. You won't always be around to come to my defense."

His lips spread, showing even white teeth in a cocky grin. "Does that mean you want me to hang out, keep an eye on you?"

Heat burned her cheeks again. "I… It just means." She swallowed hard. Why was she so flustered? "I just meant I should fight my own battles."

"Ah, One of those."

"One of those?"

"Feminists."

Feminists? Did he know this was the twenty-first century? What female wasn't something of a feminist?

35

She opened her mouth to retort, but it occurred to her that ever since she'd gotten her butt chewed, she'd been standing there, talking, still not doing her job. Not exactly the best way to get in her boss's good graces.

"Excuse me. I need to go back to work. And thanks. Really."

He inclined his head. "Any time. *Really*. By the way, I'm Eli Barkley." He took her hand and shook it, although it was more a caress than a handshake. Before she had time to figure out how he'd accomplished that, he dropped his hold. "Nice to meet you, Liberty Delacort."

"How did you…?" Never mind. It didn't matter how he knew her last name. He'd probably heard from Ryan or Bianca, or any of the other employees here. It probably wasn't every day an Okie pulled up roots and moved to Sang Croc.

Throughout the remainder of the shift, Eli stayed. He sat on a bar stool, sipping a drink, seeming to watch her every move. Making her a nervous wreck, which was probably why she dropped an entire tray of drinks on a table of customers. She felt like bursting into tears, but instead, she apologized over and over, handing them clean dry hand towels, sopping up the mess as best she could. Luckily, they were a table of four men, who were well on their way to being soused, so they took it in stride, even laughing and making jokes about it.

Jerome was waiting for her in the doorway of the kitchen, hands on hips, his broad face red and purple.

"I'm so, so, sorry." She tried hard to keep tears out of her voice, but failed. "There's no excuse for that. Are you firing me?"

He shot a glance to where Eli sat at the bar,

watching.

He gritted his teeth. "Don't worry about it. People make mistakes. Just try to be more careful."

She nodded. She would probably feel better if he had fired her. The only reason he was being cool about it was because he was afraid of this Eli guy.

Her tables were all taken care of for the moment, so she headed to where Eli sat at the bar.

"Listen, I don't mean to sound ungrateful, and I know you were trying to help, but I don't want my boss treating me different because he's apparently afraid of you. Besides, you being here is making me kind of nervous."

He brought the glass to his lips took a drink, then sat it down and leaned toward her like they shared some kind of secret. "How come I make you nervous?"

Her heart slowed, then sped up so fast, it stole her ability to speak. Finally, she managed to push words past her clogged throat. "Because you're staring at me."

He downed the remainder of his drink. "I'll go." He stood and tossed a twenty on the bar. He was so close to her now, their bodies nearly touched. "But even after I'm gone, you'll be thinking about me."

She didn't reply. He moved across the floor in long, lazy strides, then disappeared through the door. She couldn't keep a grin from emerging. And he was right, hours after he was gone, she was still thinking about him.

****

Kadin stood on the perimeter of The Perfect Getaway's patio. An older couple with a thin, long-legged blonde girl exited the restaurant. His gaze followed the girl. Barely a teenager, he was guessing. Young meat. He inhaled deeply. He could smell her from here. Did she taste as good as she smelled? Her fresh, warm, young blood…. He swallowed back saliva and forced himself to remain where he was. Too many people around, too many tourists to witness his feeding frenzy. Restraint—that was the hardest part. But if he and his kind lost control and drove the tourists away, the only humans left would be the locals. Not only did they know better than to venture out during a full moon, after a while, they would all be dead or turned, then he'd be stuck with nothing but animals for sustenance.

He brought his attention back to the window of the tiki bar just in time to see the new girl pass by. Her thick, glorious, chestnut hair was pinned back, exposing the line of slender neck… the faint blue tinge of her carotid artery. He licked his lips. He could almost smell her blood, almost feel his teeth sinking into her soft flesh…

The skin on his face tightened, and his eyes burned. He took a deep breath and forced calm to possess him. The bimbo he'd brought along stood behind him holding onto his hand so tightly, if he were human, his bones might shatter. He couldn't let the girl see him like that— see the real him. She might not put two and two together and figure out he was a vampire—hell, she might not put two and two together and come up with four—but she would know something was amiss. She'd run screaming from him, and the crowd gathered on the tiki patio would come to investigate. Damned inconvenient.

He tore his gaze from the new, tasty looking treat. For now. He'd be back to her, though. Eli seemed to have taken an interest. Intriguing. Nothing more fun than playing with Eli's toys.

The bimbo broke into his thoughts. "Why can't we go up and have a drink?" she whined.

Like he hadn't told her a dozen times, he said, "I don't like crowds. I'd rather be alone with you." Hopefully, she wouldn't ask why they were skulking around instead of going to his place, or her hotel room, where they could really be alone. Even as dumb as she was, that question would no doubt occur to her eventually.

She giggled. "I'd rather be alone with you too. I love the way your hair feels. All spiky and stiff. I wonder if another part of you is just as stiff," she purred as she ran a hand through his hair, then down his jaw, over the tattoo.

He cringed with revulsion. Why had he picked her of all the delectable tourists? She was attractive, sure, but her touch, her voice, grated on his last nerve. Truth was, he was feeling lazy tonight. She'd been easy prey. They didn't come much more gullible than... Christ. He couldn't even remember her name. Oh yeah. Marnie.

Her whiny voice intruded on his thoughts. "Want to go to the beach tomorrow?"

He flicked a glance at her and shook his head. "I'm afraid I'm not much for beaches."

"But you live on this beautiful island."

He grinned. "I'm more of a night life kind of guy."

She pressed her body against his. "But wouldn't you like to see me in a bikini?"

"I can see you completely naked right now if I want."

Her brows rose. "Oh, you think so?"

He inclined his head in a slight nod. "Take off your clothes."

She giggled again, but it sounded shaky this time. "No."

He captured her gaze with his, stared for a few seconds until he saw that glazed over look—the even more glazed over look than she normally wore—and commanded softly, "Marnie, take off your clothes."

She kept her eyes locked on his and slowly removed her clothing, including the thong panties. She wrapped her arms around her body, shivering, even though the breeze coming off the ocean wasn't all that chilly.

He didn't bother to look at her nude body. His interest ended at the base of her neck… where the vein pulsed just below the surface of her skin.

"You won't remember what happens next. You won't know how you got those marks on your neck. You'll wear a bandage. You'll tell anyone who asks that you're hiding a hickey."

"Hiding a hickey." Her voice was flat as she repeated his words.

He opened his mouth and protracted his fangs. Her eyes widened, but before she had time to react, he bent his head forward. His fangs pierced the flesh of her neck, broke the artery wall. Sweet, hot blood flowed from her into him. He moaned with satisfaction, sucking greedily, forcing himself to only take so much… not enough to drain her… but God, it was hard to stop. Her whimper was part pain, part ecstasy. Her eyes drifted shut, and she went limp in his arms. He continued to drink, but the image that surfaced in his mind was that of the new girl… Eli's prize.

****

Liberty twisted her hands nervously in her lap and shot Ryan a glance from the passenger seat. It was Friday night and the two of them, along with Bianca who sat in the back seat, were on their way to a party. Apparently it wasn't a date. Otherwise, he wouldn't have brought his sister, right?

Earlier in the week, Ryan and Bianca had both invited her. So no, not a date.

"It's at Eli's house," Ryan had said. "His parties are choice."

Eli hadn't been back in the bar since that first night, but she'd found herself watching for him ever since. Pathetic, but she couldn't help it. Something about him had been so… different… exciting. She'd gone out with Cam for four years, and never come close to feeling that tingle she'd felt when Eli looked at her. Spoke to her in that deep, husky tone. Even as hot as Ryan was, and as much as she was starting to like him, her reaction to him wasn't the same fist in the gut, blood singing, knee quivering response Eli elicited.

"We're here."

Ryan's words brought her back to the present, but did nothing to ease the butterflies scrambling around in her stomach. *Here* meant Eli's house, and he was the source of those butterflies.

She stepped out of the car, smoothing her shirt, tugging it up a little so her boobs didn't spill out. She'd dressed with extra care. Eli would see her in something other than her uniform, and she wanted to look her best. She'd worn a shimmery royal blue shirt that scooped low in the back, leaving her bare to the waist, with skinny jeans and sparkly silver heels that were so spiky, she'd probably fall on her butt before the night was over. The shoes were sexy enough that she was willing to take the risk.

A crescent shaped moon floated in the black sky between two palm trees. She, Bianca, and Ryan traversed their way up a long drive past several vehicles. Eli must throw awesome parties. He'd certainly attracted a crowd.

The house was more of a hut. A large hut, but with the thatch roof and straw covered siding, a hut was the only way to describe it. Loud music and laughter poured into the night air, growing in volume the closer they got.

Strings of sparkling white lights draped the trees in the yard. Bodies spilled outside the door. Nearly everyone they passed held a drink. A few of them held joints. Ryan took hold of her hand, guiding her through the throng of people.

"Ryan, you came." She recognized Eli's voice before she saw him. Her heart crawled up into her throat when his eyes cut to her. "And you brought a guest." He smiled and took the hand Ryan wasn't holding. Again, it was more of a caress than a shake. He held on longer this time. His skin was cool to the touch, but somehow sent warmth coursing through her. "Welcome to my home."

She took in a breath and let it out slowly. She had to get ahold of herself. Why did the slightest look, the merest touch from him make her quiver? "Thank you for having me."

"Not at all. I'm happy to—have you." He put a slight emphasis on 'have.' Did everything he did or said have some kind of hidden meaning or was that just her overactive imagination?

Ryan's grip tightened on her hand. If one of them didn't let go, she was going to have a pretty uncomfortable—not to mention, restricted—evening.

Eli glanced down to where Ryan held on to her and quirked a corner of his mouth. He slowly slid his hand along the length of hers, then released it.

Ryan scowled. "Let's go get something to drink."

She let him tug her away, but couldn't resist a quick peek over her shoulder. Eli was watching. He lifted his drink in a salute and brought it to his lips. Her heart raced, and blood pumped through her veins so hard she could feel it thrumming in her ears. What the hell? What was it about him that could have that effect? Like the effect she'd read about in romance novels…

Ugh. So not true. He was just hot… charming. He'd rescued her from her ogre of a boss, after all. She was vulnerable right now and…

"So, what would you like? We have beer, punch, vodka, all kinds of shots, anything you can imagine."

"I'll take a beer, please."

Ryan poured from a keg into a plastic blue cup and handed it to her. She took a sip and frowned at the bitter taste that coated her tongue. She'd never cared that much for beer, but since she wasn't much of a drinker and was in a strange, new place with people she barely knew, she should probably stick with something mild.

Bianca came up and took her arm. "Come on, I'll show you around. Let me borrow her for a tic, Ryan."

She didn't give him a chance to respond before whisking Liberty away. They approached a guy and girl standing next to the punch bowl.

"Diego, Nadia, this is Liberty," Bianca said. "She's new to the island."

Diego had brooding features, thick, dark eyebrows and close-cropped black hair. "Nice to meet you." He didn't sound like he meant it, and he didn't shake her hand.

Nadia's mouth tightened in disapproval, but she took Liberty's hand. "I know who you are. I work at Perfect Getaway."

"Oh?" Liberty was sure she would have noticed her. She had a unique and unforgettable beauty, with skin the color of a mocha latte and startling light blue eyes.

"We haven't worked together yet, but I heard about you."

Liberty detected the hint of a Jamaican accent and a hint of bitterness in her tone. The two seemed to dislike her without ever having met her. She was glad when Bianca moved away, introducing her to more people who were friendlier.

"Is there a reason Diego and Nadia don't like me?" Liberty asked when there was a lull in the introductions.

Bianca shrugged. "They don't care for strangers in general. They're okay with tourists, but you make them uncomfortable. Coming from a faraway place, infiltrating our world."

"Infiltrating? I—I wasn't trying to…"

Bianca laughed. "I didn't mean that as a bad thing. I'm glad to have met you. Glad to be working with you. Those two will come around."

Liberty nodded, but couldn't help thinking—like so many other things she'd heard since she arrived—there was more to their attitude than Bianca was telling her.

After a few minutes, the faces and names seemed to run together. Bodies were packed so tightly inside the sparsely furnished living room, Liberty was starting to feel claustrophobic.

She leaned toward Bianca so she could hear her over "Use Somebody" by Kings of Leon blasting from the stereo. "I need some air."

"You okay?" Bianca's pretty face scrunched up in concern.

"Yeah, sure. Just kind of crowded in here."

Liberty sipped from the still nearly full cup of beer and wandered toward a row of trees. She glanced around for Ryan, but didn't see him. She'd catch up with him later. For now, she needed a breather.

The water was no more than twenty feet beyond where she stood. Ripples moved over the dark blue glassy surface. She looked up at the sky. Like the water, it was calming, beautiful, an inky black broken only by the shine of the moon. The faint sounds of the party drifted to her…music, laughter, but for the most part, there was peace.

A flapping noise drew her attention. At first, she thought they were birds, then horror struck when she realized they were… bats. A yelp escaped her throat, and she shuddered. Bats? *You have got to be kidding me.* She backed away, turning to head back to the party.

"Do bats frighten you?"

She jumped at the sound of Eli's voice. She'd been so focused on the disgusting creatures, she hadn't noticed his arrival.

She let out a shaky laugh. "I— They, uh, startled me. They're a little creepy. Not exactly something you see every day. At least not where I come from."

"And where do you come from, lovely Liberty?"

Her throat went dry, and she attempted a swallow. "Uhm. Newcastle, Oklahoma. It's a small town. You've probably never heard of it."

"Hmmm. I've never had—*met*—anyone from Oklahoma before." His eyes danced devilishly. "Here." He handed her a wine glass. In his other hand he held an amber-colored drink.

"What is this for?"

"It's wine. I saw you turn up your cute little nose

every time you took a sip of beer."

He'd been watching her? Again. She wasn't sure whether to be flattered or insulted. "Thank you."

He took the plastic cup from her hand and tossed it away. "Don't worry about the littering. I'll clean all this up later."

She nodded, at a loss for a response that wouldn't sound like silly babbling. He was no doubt using his practiced charm on her, but it was working. She felt… special… wanted.

To cover her nervousness, she took a sip from the glass. The wine was tart with a hint of sweetness. Similar to what Antoine had served. She liked it. Maybe she would be more of a drinker now that she'd discovered white wine.

"Thanks. This is delicious. And it's not red. Good choice."

"Once in a while, I make good choices. You don't like red?"

She wasn't about to tell him about her blood phobia, or that she couldn't eat or drink anything red. How lame would that sound? "I heard red wine is bitter."

"You should never have bitterness in your life." His gaze roamed down to her spiky heels, then slowly moved back up to her face. "Have I told you that you look especially gorgeous this evening?"

She shook her head and gulped more of the wine. "Th—thank you."

He smiled. "Do compliments make you uncomfortable?"

"No. I'm just not used to…" she trailed off helplessly.

Not used to devastatingly hot guys coming on to

her? That pretty much summed it up. Cam was hot, there was no doubt about it, but he couldn't come close to Eli's sexiness. The way he spoke, the way he moved, the way he seemed to look into her very soul with those hypnotic eyes…

Though the music coming from the party was muted, she recognized an Elvis Presley song, "One Night." She grinned at Eli. "You like Elvis Presley? Isn't he a little before your time?"

His lips twitched with amusement and he shrugged. "You might say I'm an old soul."

"Yeah, me too." Sometimes she felt way older than her years. But not now. Now she felt young and…happy.

She lifted the cup to take another drink, but it was empty. She hadn't realized she'd drunk so much so fast. Her head swam with a slight case of dizziness. But she liked it. It made her feel relaxed. Free. Liberated. *Liberated Liberty.* She giggled.

"You okay?" He brushed a strand of hair out of her face. His touch ignited her insides, and heat flooded her body.

"I'm fine. Awesome, as a matter of fact."

He moved closer until only a hint of space separated their bodies. "Liberty?" His raspy voice was like a caress over her flesh. A breeze wafted over her bare back, and she shivered. She waited breathlessly for his next words, his next move. "You find me irresistible," he whispered, his gaze never leaving hers. "You're helpless to deny me anything. Your knees are weak." He stroked his finger over her shoulder, letting them trail down to the center of her chest, just above her breasts. "Your heart is pounding for me right now. All you can think about is what it would feel like to kiss me."

She licked her lips, wishing her glass wasn't empty. Her mouth was so dry, she couldn't speak. But oh wow… was he ever right. She didn't even mind his aggressive, unusual approach. Something about the atmosphere, about leaving behind the trappings of home. The memories of what Cam and Alyssa had done made her reckless. She took his glass from his hand without breaking eye contact. His eyebrows rose as he watched her take a sip of the strong liquor, whatever it was. It burned her throat and eyes, but she resisted the urge to cough. It had done the trick, and she was able to whisper, "Yes."

The corner of his mouth quirked. He moved closer, brushed his lips along hers, just a tease. That was it? That was the kiss? She bit back a groan of frustration. Her body ached with disappointment. But he moved toward her again, his eyes searching, his lips a hairsbreadth from hers. He stroked a hand down the side of her neck. His touch sent a flash of fire through her veins. She nearly moaned in anticipation, in yearning to feel his mouth, firm and hot against hers. She braced herself. Something primitive deep within told her this would be the kiss to rival any other. She swayed, her lids drifting shut, every nerve in her body tingling…

A scream tore through the night, breaking the spell. Liberty's eyes flew open, and she gasped.

Eli stepped back. "Dammit," he bit out. He cupped her cheek in his hand. "Don't forget where we were."

Then he was gone. She could barely feel her legs. Were they still supporting her? What the hell had just happened?

She shook her head, then followed the sound of excited voices where the scream had originated.

A group of people had gathered around a gazebo at the back of the house.

Liberty pushed her way through the crowd. Ryan knelt in the center of the gazebo next to a bench where a girl lay still. Her skin was as white as the moon, blank eyes staring at the midnight sky.

Liberty was afraid to look, but somehow couldn't help herself. She scanned the girl's body from head to toe. No blood. Good, that was a good sign, right? But the girl looked so… dead.

"Son of a bitch," a male voice shouted. "She's been drained."

Chapter 4

"Drained?" Liberty demanded of Ryan the next day at work. She hadn't had a chance to confront him the night before. He'd waited with the body for the police to arrive and had Bianca take her home. Liberty had asked Bianca questions, but she'd denied knowing anything. Liberty didn't believe her. "What do they mean, drained?"

Ryan shrugged, not meeting her eyes. "They just meant she was gone... drained of life."

"Kind of a poetic way to put it in a moment of panic wouldn't you say?"

Ryan tried for a casual shrug. "I'm from Australia, love. Everything sounds poetic to me."

"Come on. How did she die? I didn't see any blood... no injury. What happened to her?"

Ryan busied himself making drinks, his back to her. "I guess they'll find out in the autopsy."

Liberty blew out a frustrated sigh. Her section was full. She didn't have time for this. But later. Yes, later, she'd force some answers out of him, one way or the other.

By the time the day ended, Liberty discovered she'd either overestimated her powers of persuasion or underestimated Ryan's power of evasion. Either way, she didn't get the answers she wanted.

Ryan drove her home, still refusing to satisfy her

curiosity. Maybe she *would* have to wait until after the autopsy, see it on the news. Her newfound friends certainly weren't very helpful.

She changed out of her uniform and headed to Victor's room. Antoine had suggested it, said he'd bring dinner up to her. He agreed that she needed to work on establishing some kind of relationship, of getting to know her father.

Victor lifted his head from the pillow when she entered, then frowned and let it drop back.

Undeterred, she moved to the side of the bed. "I know you don't want me here, but I'm going to spend as much time with you as I can. I've missed out on a whole lifetime."

"It's not safe for you here."

"You've said that already. I know. I just don't know why. But the thing is, I'm staying on the island no matter what. So, you can ignore me and rob me of whatever time you have left, or you can spend time with me, make up for the years I lost. Either way, the level of danger remains the same. So, what's it going to be?"

He blinked rapidly, but his attempts to fight back tears failed. Moisture shimmered in his eyes and Liberty felt a sting in her own.

"I've grieved for you all these years. I only want you to leave for your own safety. I'd like nothing more than to spend my remaining days getting to know you."

Days? Surely they had more than just days. She wasn't ready to give him up just yet.

She sat on the side of his bed, and they fell easily into conversation, although the topics were mundane. He wouldn't discuss the reason he feared for her so much.

"Don't you know I'll find out soon enough? After

you're… gone." She could barely say the word. She definitely couldn't bring herself to say the 'D' word.

"I'm hoping you'll get some sense and leave before that happens." A smile accompanied the words, but she detected the truth behind them. "In the meantime, the less you know, the better. For your own safety."

Their conversation was interrupted by Antoine. He brought in their dinner—roast chicken, yams, and fresh pineapple—and along with it, a brown leather photo album.

"I thought you two might want to look through this."

He laid the album on the bed next to Victor.

"Thank you, Antoine." Liberty smiled her appreciation. She'd offered on several occasions to help with the cooking and serving, but Antoine had insisted on doing it himself. Maybe he'd guessed how much she sucked at cooking. Her mom wasn't much of a cook either. Her whole life they'd eaten mostly fast food or soup and sandwiches. Liberty had learned to make a killer grilled cheese.

After dinner, Victor picked up the album. His face softened, his eyes taking on a faraway look. He turned the album to where she could see the pages. He pointed at a photo of him and a little girl—she still couldn't quite believe that she was the child in the photos—next to a boat. In the photo, she held a fish aloft.

"You were my little fisherman buddy. We had a lot of good times together. You followed me around like a puppy."

The poignancy of the memory, just out of her grasp, warred with her confusion and pain. "But you sent me away."

"It became too dangerous for you here."

"My mother, even now, insists she doesn't know you. That she's never been to this island. Why would she do that?"

He closed the album and turned to stare out the window. Night had fallen and the three quarter moon hung just below the top edge of the window.

"She's afraid for you, just as I am."

"But once she saw I was determined to come, she continued to lie."

He shrugged, still not looking at her. "Maybe she would rather forget. Maybe she's convinced herself it never happened."

"Were you and my mom in love?"

He turned back to face her. A smile softened his features. "I loved her very much. I think she loved me, too. I wish she could at least remember that."

"She must remember. It makes no sense that she could erase something like that from her mind."

"This island can bring out odd behavior."

Liberty pushed off the side of the bed and stood, crossing her arms. "I'm so tired of all the secrets, the evasions. Does whatever you're hiding have anything to do with what happened to the girl at the party?"

"What girl?"

"I went to Eli Barkley's party last night. A girl was killed. Someone said she was drained."

His eyes widened. "What?" His face had grown even paler. "While you were at the party?"

Liberty nodded. "Why would they say she was drained?"

He closed his eyes and let his head fall back on the pillows. "I'm very tired. Maybe you should go now."

"Not until you tell me what it means. I was there. It

could have been me. If it has something to do with what you're hiding from me, don't you think it's time you told me the truth?"

"She's right, you know."

Liberty turned to see Antoine standing in the doorway.

He moved farther into the room. "You know she'll be needed."

Victor glared at him. "She's not to become involved. She can't."

"Involved in what?" Liberty demanded. "Quit acting like I'm not here."

Still ignoring her, Antoine said, "You would have an entire society perish to protect one person?"

Victor's eyes flashed with more life than she'd seen since she'd met him. "I'd sacrifice the world to protect my daughter."

****

That night, Liberty couldn't sleep. Every time she closed her eyes, she saw the girl—the *dead* girl. It was so hard to believe. And so sad. Just a few moments before, she'd been alive, having fun with her friends, then just… gone. How could life be so fragile? How had she died? Right there at the party? The questions tumbled around in her brain, along with images of the girl's still, pale body. Why wouldn't anyone talk to her?

Maybe she hadn't asked the right person. Although she'd only seen him a few times, she could tell that Eli had a reckless streak. She saw it in his eyes, in the way he carried himself. He would talk to her.

She quietly climbed from her bed and slipped on jeans and a pink V neck shirt.

It wasn't until she had stealthily made her way

through the house and outside that it occurred to her, how would she get there? Ryan had been her ride everywhere she'd gone up to this point. Her U.S. driver's license was valid on the island, and Antoine had offered to let her drive Victor's car, but she wasn't ready to attempt navigating the narrow windy roads, especially when she discovered Victor's car was a Porsche. She couldn't imagine crashing such an expensive car.

Making a decision, she headed toward the road on foot. Eli's house wasn't that far. She could walk. Although it was rude to go to someone's house this late at night, uninvited, she had a feeling Eli didn't follow the rules of polite society. And it was unlikely he'd be asleep. He struck her as someone who was late to bed and late to rise.

The distance was farther than she realized. She'd walked what she was certain had to be more than a mile, and was beginning to wonder if she'd gone the wrong way, when she finally reached his house.

A dim light glowed in the living room window. Maybe he wasn't alone. Was he with a girl? A twinge of something more than unease pricked her heart—it wasn't jealousy, was it? Why should she be jealous? She barely knew him. Maybe rather than jealousy, it was a fierce desire to be the one he was holding… touching… the one who was feeling those sensuous lips skating along her flesh…

She shivered. *Pretty lusty thoughts for a virgin, Liberty.* She shook the images away. She seriously needed to chill.

She made her way to the door and started to knock, then paused. Maybe she should take a quick peek before she knocked and embarrassed them both. The curtain on the window in the door was pulled back. She lifted to her tiptoes and peered in the window. At first she saw nothing. Then her gaze moved to the far end of the room.

Eli's back was to her. He had a woman pressed against the wall, his head bent to her neck. The woman's auburn hair was tangled around her head, her eyes closed, a look of rapture on her face. Who could blame her? Liberty had felt just a hint of his sensual touch and nearly melted into the ground. What would it feel like to have him that close? Doing the things he was doing—or about to do—to that woman? Heat burned through her blood and flushed her cheeks. She swallowed hard. She couldn't stop looking. The sight sickened her while at the same time, sent an odd yearning deep in her belly.

No. She wouldn't watch like some pervert.

She braced her hands on the door, intending to step back. Before she could, Eli lifted his head and whipped it toward her. He couldn't have heard her, could he? She'd barely made a sound. Maybe he just sensed—

Her thoughts ceased when she took a closer look at Eli's face. He stood in place, breathing heavily. She narrowed her eyes. *God. No.*

His features were somehow distorted, his skin had a gray cast and looked… crumpled. His eyes glowed red. Something dark and liquid—blood?—was smeared around his mouth, dripped off his… *fangs?*

"No!" She let out the cry before she could stop herself, then clamped a hand over her mouth.

Backing from the door, she shook her head violently from side to side. It couldn't be. No way. She had to have imagined it.

A sound at the door told her Eli was coming out. She turned and fled. Her tennis shoes slapped the ground, the

noise reverberating in her ears along with the word—
vampire… vampire… vampire. Oh my God. Vampire…
Bats… *Drained…*

A hand landed on her arm. She screamed and
stumbled, nearly falling to the ground. Eli pulled her up
and whirled her around to face him.

"Let me go!" Terror strangled her vocal cords. She
jerked at his hold, but couldn't budge him. His face was
back to normal except for the red eyes. Trembles shook
her body.

"Calm down," he said, so softly she almost didn't
hear him.

He wiped blood from his mouth. *Blood.* Oh God.

Nausea surfaced in her throat. She clutched her
stomach, afraid she was going to throw up.

"Don't touch me." Her voice came out hoarse from
her raw throat. She jerked her arm again, and this time
he released her.

He held his hands out. "Liberty. Let me explain—"

"Explain what? That you're a—a vampire?" She
wrapped her arms around her body and backed away.
"How is that even possible?"

Eli squeezed his eyes shut. When he opened them,
the red was gone, and they glinted their usual silvery
blue. The moonlight reflecting in them made them look
like Christmas tinsel.

"It is what it is, sweetheart." A muscle ticked in his
clenched jaw. "I'm a vampire."

Hc took a step toward her, and she took a step back.
"Stay away from me."

He shrugged. "You're the one who came to my
house in the middle of the night." He was still moving
slowly toward her. His eyes roamed over her body. "I

can only guess why. " His voice was low, hypnotic. He jerked his head toward his house. "I can send her packing if you'd like."

"She—she's not dead?"

His mouth curved in a slow smile. "Did she look dead? I assure you, a killing was not what you interrupted."

Revulsion washed through her body and clogged her chest. "I can only imagine."

"You don't have to—imagine, that is. Come back with me." He lifted a hand toward her. "I promise not to puncture the skin."

She slapped his hand away. "You disgust me." Her heart froze. Where had she gotten the nerve to talk to a vampire like that? He could eat her… drain her.

Drain her… that's what had happened to the girl at the party. She'd been attacked by a vampire. Not Eli. He'd been with Liberty. So, there were more of them. How many? Did Ryan know about the vampires? She had to warn him…

Thoughts tumbled on top of one another, but none of them made sense. Her brain felt numb and too full, like it was stuffed with cotton. Dizziness assailed her. She swayed. Eli stepped forward and took hold of her elbow. "Come on, let's get you home."

She jerked away. "I can get home on my own."

"Did you walk here?"

She didn't respond.

He smiled. "Now that you know there are vampires… and surely you don't think I'm the only one. Are you really going to walk a mile in the dark, alone?"

She tightened her lips and backed away.

He slowly advanced. "If I wanted to… eat you… I

wou0ld do it now. I wouldn't have to trick you into getting into the car with me."

Because she knew he was right. And because she damn sure didn't want to run into an entire flock of vampires, she gave a short nod. He gestured with his hand for her to precede him. She marched to his car, her back tensing at the thought of him being behind her. In the dark. Where he could leap on her at any moment. She drew in a deep breath and shook off the thought. As he'd said, if he wanted to attack her, he would have already done it.

She climbed into a sleek black Corvette. He got into the driver's side, and she scrunched against the door, looking out the window. During the drive, he tried to talk to her, but she ignored him. She was freaking out. She didn't want to hear anything he had to say, although admittedly, she had a thousand questions. But she couldn't stand to hear answers tonight. And not from him. Ever.

****

Liberty didn't close her eyes that night. She roamed the house until the sun rose. A realization came to her in the wee hours. Van Helsing... she'd heard that name. Vampire hunter. Was her father a vampire hunter? Was she? Was that her destiny?

Not long after sunrise, Antoine entered the kitchen where she sat staring into a cup of coffee.

Without lifting her head, she said, "Did you know about the vampires?"

Silence greeted her, then, "How did you find out?"

Her mind flashed to what she'd witnessed at Eli's house. She squeezed her eyes shut and shoved the memory away. "It doesn't matter. I know. I'm taking the next flight out."

"I understand your fear, but—"

She jerked her head up to look at him. "You must *not* understand or you'd never have brought me here. My father was right in trying to protect me. Good God, this place is crawling with monsters." She'd adlibbed the 'crawling' part. She had no idea how many vampires there were, but one was too many.

He settled at the table next to her and linked his hands on the surface. "I told you it was your destiny. I had my reasons."

She barked a bitter laugh. "My destiny is to be drained by a vampire?"

"That's not going to happen."

"How do you know?"

She wanted him to give her an answer that would ease her anxiety. An answer that would make her stay. Even with the discovery of the vampires, she was reluctant to leave. Go back to what? A mother who'd lied to her. A cheating ex-boyfriend and ex best friend? The island made her feel more alive, more independent than she'd ever thought possible. Besides, she was getting to know the father she'd been cheated out of.

"I know. Trust me."

She laughed. "Right. Trust someone who brought me here under false pretenses?"

"I never lied to you. I said your father was dying. That your destiny awaits. Those were both truths." His gaze captured hers. "No matter what you think of me at this moment, I want you to understand something. I will never lie to you. Never. Understand?"

She didn't give him the satisfaction of agreeing, but for some reason, she believed him. "I want to see my father."

"He is resting. He had a difficult night. I am afraid his time is near."

"No!" After everything she'd learned, after all she'd gone through to get here. She couldn't lose him. Not yet.

She pushed away from the table and ran upstairs. As soon as she opened the door, she heard his labored breathing.

Silently, she moved to the bed. His eyes fluttered open, and he gave a weak smile. "My sweet Liberty."

"How are you?" He looked so frail, so weak and vulnerable.

"I'm okay. Not bad." He dragged his hand from the bed and cupped her cheek. "I don't know how much time I have left. I want you to know, even though I fear for you. I'm glad I got to know you before I—"

"No. You have time. Plenty of time."

He smiled. "Yes. Plenty of time."

She sat next to him on the bed. "I need to ask you something. I think I know why you're so afraid for me to be here."

"Oh?"

"The vampires."

He drew in an audible gasp. "How—how did you find out? Did Antoine tell you? I'll have his head."

"No. Not Antoine. It's not important how I found out." She couldn't stand the thought of replaying what she'd seen. "But I *do* know. Don't you think it would have been better if you had told me? Being in the dark isn't being safe."

"I'm sorry. Maybe so. But I'd hoped you'd leave without ever finding out."

"And that's why you sent me away when I was a

child. You feared for my safety."

He nodded. A weary sigh escaped him, and he took her hand. "I fell in love with your mother while she was here on vacation. I knew better, but I couldn't resist the idea of a family. A normal life. It worked for a while, too. Until…" He closed his eyes and shook his head.

"Until what?" she prodded. She had to know. Everything.

"You were barely three years old. You witnessed an attack. There was so much carnage. So much blood."

"What attack? Who?" Why couldn't she remember? Of course, she'd been very young. And it had to have been traumatic. All the blood… now it made sense. Her fear of blood. Was that why?

"You didn't know them. They were tourists. You and I went out for ice cream one evening. Two vampires came into the store." He opened his eyes and looked at her. "I'd rather not help you relive the details. If you've forgotten, that's best. It was then I knew. I had to get you and your mother away."

"My mother. Why does she pretend not to remember? She could have at least told me part of the truth. Does she know about the vampires?"

"She did. At one time."

"I don't understand."

He took hold of her hand. "I'm very tired, Liberty. I hoped you would never find out about the vampires. But you have. Please don't ask any more questions. After I'm gone, you'll learn more than I ever wanted you to. This is not what I'd hoped would be your future. But for now, for the time I have left, let's please not talk about it anymore."

Reluctantly, she nodded. She had to know, but he

was right. She didn't want to upset him or wear him out. She wanted to enjoy the time they had together… however long that would be.

"Okay. Sure. I won't ask any more of you."

"One thing I want you to know is, for the past fifteen years, not a day went by that I didn't think about you, that I didn't miss you, that I didn't love you. And now that I've gotten you back, I don't want to leave you."

"I don't want you to," she said through her tears. "You have time. I know it. You just need some rest. I'll have Antoine call the doctor."

"He's on his way," Antoine said from where he stood in the open doorway. She hadn't known he'd followed her up, but was glad he had.

"I'm not going anywhere just yet." Victor's voice was weak, exhausted. "We have time."

She nodded and held her father's hand until the doctor arrived. She and Antoine waited outside Victor's door.

Antoine's stoic face was drawn in worry. They didn't speak. If they had, she would have quizzed him further about the vampires. But now wasn't the time.

Victor's door opened, and the doctor stepped out. She rushed to him. "How is he? It's not… he's not…"

Doctor Lemanu was a short Tahitian man with kind eyes and ageless features. He shook his head. "He is weak, but he has a bit of time left." He spoke in heavily accented but clear English. "Do not excite him. Just enjoy the time you have together."

She nodded. "I'm scheduled to work, but I don't want to leave him if he's…"

"Go to work, child." He patted her cheek. "Put it out of your mind. He has time."

Chapter 5

Work was a disaster. Liberty made so many mistakes; she just knew Jerome would fire her. Oh wait, no he wouldn't. A freakin' vampire had threatened him. He'd probably let Hitler work here under those conditions. Hannah had come in to return the necklace, and Liberty barely had time to speak two words to her.

She cringed after the fourth table of customers yelled at her for getting their order wrong. She apologized profusely, but they demanded to see the manager. For God's sake, how was she supposed to concentrate when her father, who she'd only just started getting to know, was at death's door? Not to mention she'd just discovered the existence of vampires, and with only a little coaxing, would have willingly given her virginity to one. *He was this close to your lips, your neck, he could have…* She swallowed back a rush of bile. *Get it out of your mind. Focus.*

The end of her shift finally came, and Bianca gave her a ride home. Ryan was off tonight. She would go straight to her father's room. He might be asleep, but she could at least look in on him. Even though he was as much to blame for the deception that had been her whole life, not to mention the deception about vampires, she couldn't place any blame on him. Not in his terminal condition. She'd reserve her resentment and anger for the living, including her mother, who'd made Liberty's

64

entire existence one big fat lie.

She frowned at Ryan's car parked in the driveway. What was he doing here?

"Thank you," she mumbled to Bianca. She jumped from the car and raced through the door. Antoine was nowhere to be seen, nor was Ryan.

Were they in with her father? Had something happened? Panic propelled her up the stairs. She was breathing heavily by the time she reached the top. Victor's door stood open. Her steps slowed, as if her feet knew she wanted to put off whatever was waiting as long as she could.

She stepped inside the door and sucked in a breath. Not only were Ryan and Antoine standing by his bed, Eli was there too. He lifted his head and met her gaze. Panic gripped her, and she backed up a step. But something about his demeanor… his eyes… were those tears? She swallowed her misgivings, worry for her father overtaking her fear.

She rushed to his bed. His eyes were closed, his chest still. "Dad?" She pushed past Ryan and Eli and took Victor's hand. His face was relaxed, his chest not moving. "Dad? Please open your eyes. Please!"

She whirled to the others. "Someone, do something." Anguish pierced her chest. "Where's the doctor? He needs the doctor."

"It is too late," Antoine said quietly. "The doctor left only moments ago. Your father is gone."

"But—but he said he had time. *We* had time."

Antoine dropped his head. Ryan and Eli didn't speak. They looked on, silently waiting. For her to break down?

She choked out a sob. Grief balled up in her throat

so that the words came out a strangled whisper. "He sent me away on purpose."

"Your father did not wish for you to see him take his last breath."

So, he'd cheated her out of a chance to say goodbye, too. She turned back to the bed. Her knees nearly gave out, and her body sagged. A hand reached out and took hold of her arm. She wasn't sure if it was Ryan or Eli, but she shook it off.

She sank to the edge of the bed and lay across her father's chest. "I love you, Daddy," she whispered.

Tears flowed like a faucet she couldn't shut off. She wept for the loss of the man she barely knew, but had loved as much as any daughter could love a father. She wept for her mother who she needed right now more than she'd ever needed her. And she wept for herself. For all she'd lost as a child and could never get back.

****

Liberty didn't know how long she'd cried, but when she lifted her head, the others were gone. She found them downstairs in the library.

Antoine handed her a high ball glass filled with clear liquid. Vodka? She shook her head. "None for me."

"She likes white wine," Eli said.

She shot him a glare. "Does he have to be here?"

Eli sauntered closer and lowered his voice. "Do I frighten you?"

"Eli, please." Ryan spoke wearily. "Cut out the channeling Dracula bullshit and get off her. She's dealt with a lot these past few days. Give her a break."

Eli cut him a glance, then turned back to her and held her gaze for a moment before retreating to a corner of the room where he settled on a stool.

"Yes," Ryan said. "I'm afraid he does have to be here. We have things to discuss."

She turned to Ryan, "You knew, didn't you? You knew about the vampires?" A thought struck her that made her heart plummet to her stomach. "Wait, are you a...?"

Eli laughed. "Ryan, a vampire? Come now, use your head. You've seen him in the daylight. He's got a nice, sexy tan. How could he be a vampire?"

She compressed her lips and shot him another glare. She didn't want to hear from him. Didn't want to see him. And she damn sure didn't want him mocking her.

"Everyone on the island knows." Ryan brought his glass to his lips and took a long swallow. "At least the locals."

"Then how... how has the news not spread? Why wouldn't it be splashed all over the media?"

"They know tourism would die—sorry for the word choice. It's their livelihood."

She remembered the rumors she'd heard about the high mortality rate, the number of people who disappear after coming to the island. "But the mysterious deaths. Surely people would stop coming here anyway."

Eli stood and went to the bar to refill his glass. "The beauty of the island draws them. As does the promise of wealth and eternal youth."

She narrowed her eyes on him, then turned to Ryan. "Wealth and eternal youth?"

"You asked me about it when we first met," Ryan said. "The rumor about a cave that holds a stream with water that can provide eternal youth. You know, a fountain of youth, only in a cave."

"Rumor? So it isn't true?"

"The cave holds holy water."

"Holy water?"

Eli moved to stand beside her. She backed up a step. His mouth quirked. "That's right. Acid to vampires. Wouldn't you like to get your paws on that?"

She lifted her chin. "Or a cross, or garlic, or a stake."

His jaw clenched. "You wouldn't know how to use a stake if it came with an instruction manual."

Anger overtook her fear. "You don't know anything about me."

"I know you're weak, helpless. In need of protection." He took a sip from his glass. "And don't forget, you weren't exactly honest and up front with us. You never told us you were Victor's daughter."

"Antoine made me swear to keep it secret." Why was she defending herself to him?

His eyes widened. "Wait. You're a Van Helsing. You can't be mesmerized."

"Mesmerized? What do you mean?"

"Never mind." A satisfied smile curved his mouth. "But I just answered one of my questions."

His cocky grin unnerved her. "What the hell are you talking about?"

"Enough of this silly bickering," Antoine snapped. "Vampires have the power to mesmerize humans, to make them forget things, to bend them to their will."

"What does that have to do with…" Realization hit. "Was that what happened to my mother? Was she mesmerized?"

Antoine nodded. "Your father wanted her to forget all about the island. Never wanted either of you to return, to remember anything about him or this place. One of his friends—a vampire—erased your mother's memories."

Guilt squeezed her chest. Her mother hadn't lied to her. Not at all. Knowing made her want to see her mom, right now, to apologize, to hug her…

Before she could fully digest the information, Antoine continued, "Now that Mr. Van Helsing is gone, I am no longer bound to my promise. There are things you should know. Things that are expected of you as a Van Helsing."

"I've learned all I care to learn about this island and the freaks who live here. I only stayed because of my father. Now that he's—gone—I'm leaving."

"Please hear me out." His usual imperious tone had turned contrite, almost pleading.

She crossed her arms and tightened her lips, waiting expectantly.

"I am certain the Van Helsing name sounded familiar to you, although you might not have placed it, or have known it was 'that' Van Helsing even if you did."

"He was a fictitious vampire hunter."

"Not fictitious. Just as vampires are real, so are the Van Helsing hunters. You are the last in the line. That is why I brought you here. Once your father was gone, there would be no one to take up his legacy."

"And what would happen then?"

Eli spoke. "Pandemonium, anarchy, slaughter. All those pleasant things."

Antoine frowned at him then turned back to Liberty. "There is a lot you must learn, but for now, know this. On the island, there are good vampires and evil vampires." He inclined his head toward Eli. "In spite of his poor manners and dramatic, hostile posturing, Eli is one of the good ones."

"Could have fooled me," she mumbled.

Eli laughed. "Yes, but you're easily fooled."

"Enough!" Ryan shouted. "For God's sake, she needs to know what's going on, and if you two continue your schoolyard sniping, it will take days to get it out."

"Thank you, Ryan," Antoine said. "It's nice to see someone here can keep a level head. As I was saying, there are good and evil vampires. Without a Van Helsing, the evil vampires will multiply in numbers rapidly. The good vampires, the natives, the tourists, won't stand a chance."

"How can a Van Helsing stop that?"

Eli spoke. "A stake to the heart by the average Joe can kill a vampire, but if a vampire is killed by a Van Helsing, then their line is unable to procreate."

She raised her brows. "I don't get it."

He let out a heavy sigh and gave her a patronizing smile. "Since I'm the only one of the vampire persuasion in the room, I'll explain. As easily and simply as I can."

Unspoken were the words, *so even your pea brain can understand.*

"If a vampire feeds during a full moon, their victim will turn, become a vampire. In order to carry on our bloodlines, vampires are required to turn one person during a full moon. No more, no less. Otherwise, our bloodline would die out. However, there is a faction of vampires—the Evil Ones, or EO's as we've come to refer to them—whose goal is to turn as many people as possible. So needless to say, on a full moon, the town shuts down, and people stay behind closed doors. Unsuspecting tourists are often caught in the crossfire, but the locals know to keep a low profile."

"That's awful." An image of Eli—blood dripping

from his mouth—filled her head, and she swallowed back a wave of nausea. She forced herself to face him. "You turn humans into vampires? That's just... not right."

His lip curled. "Why am I not surprised you're so judgmental? If we failed to turn a human each full moon, the other vampires would by far outnumber us. You have no idea what it's like to be a vampire. No clue about our ways." His gaze traveled slowly over her body and back up to her face. "Our urges."

She crossed her arms over her breasts and met his stare, determined not to look away—not to lose a battle of wills with him. "You're right. But I know far more than I'd like to. I wish I'd never come here."

But then, you wouldn't have met your father. Would she trade that for not knowing about the vampires? Never having seen what Eli did to that poor girl? No. Truth was, she would do it all again if it meant spending even another hour with her father.

"Well, you can't *un* arrive on the island, so I guess you'll just have to deal, right? Do you want to hear how this works, or do you want to keep whining?"

She opened her mouth to offer a scathing retort, but realized Antoine and Ryan were right. She and Eli sounded like children. She'd so looked forward to turning eighteen, to becoming an adult, now it was time she started acting like one. "Please continue."

He lifted a brow as if surprised, but didn't comment on her change of attitude. "If a vampire is killed by a Van Helsing, then that vampire's entire line, anyone they ever turned or who was ever turned by anyone they've turned, etc, loses the ability to procreate—to turn a human into a vampire. So, if a Van Helsing kills enough vampires, eventually, the entire race could possibly die out."

"So, you're telling me vampires fear me?"

Ryan spoke up. "Not you, per se, but a trained Van Helsing, yes."

Antoine moved to her side and took her hands in his. "It is your destiny to take up where your father left off. His work is the only thing that has kept the Evil Ones from running rampant. Since he fell ill, they've increased in numbers. By the next full moon, who knows how many will be created."

"She can't do it," Eli snarled. "Look at her. She's small, weak. Face it, it's over." He drew in a deep breath. A suspicious glint of moisture hovered in his eyes, and his voice was hoarse—was that emotion? He pushed to his feet. "I'm out of here. You two can go on painting her a picture of unicorns and rainbows. Then watch her get herself—and no telling how many others—killed in the process. Without Van Helsing, we're screwed. It's time you 'glass half full, rose-colored glasses optimists' realized it."

He strode from the room, slamming out the front door.

Ryan shook his head. "He cared a lot about Victor. We all did. But unlike him, I'm not giving up. You can do this."

She hated to agree with Eli, but he was right. "I have no idea how to stop them, how to kill them, even if I had the stomach for it, which I don't. And even if I was staying, which I'm not."

But her words lacked conviction. They could tell, she could see it in their faces. Her heart was telling her what her brain hadn't yet accepted. If being a Van

Helsing was her destiny. If she could learn to halt the spread of evil, she would answer her calling.

After all. She was a Van Helsing.

Chapter 6

Eli tipped the glass to his lips and emptied it, then refilled it, fuller this time. What a shit load of a mess they were in. The EO's would wreak havoc now.

Liberty… she was weak, delicate, soft… He groaned and swallowed more of his drink.

Damn. He hadn't mesmerized her. She'd had all her faculties when he'd pulled his seduction routine. She'd been willing, pliant. He could have tasted her…

A thought occurred that froze his already frozen insides. Had he really tasted her… pierced her flesh… drank from her, he'd be… He shuddered and downed the drink. That would teach him to choose his flavors more carefully. Self mutilation was not on his bucket list.

But God, was she tempting. Her eyes, as green as the jungles of the island, the throaty, husky voice, her hair like silky dark caramel. He hadn't been drawn to a human this way since Christelle. *And you saw how that ended.*

Nothing to be gained by being captivated by another human. Of course, with Christelle, it was more than being captivated. For the first time, he'd known how it felt to love. He tightened his fist so hard, the glass shattered. Shards pierced his skin, bloodied his flesh, but he barely felt it. Besides, it would heal in seconds. Unlike his heart.

He pushed aside thoughts of Christelle, grabbed a

new glass, and filled it. Apparently, his mind was determined to focus on either Christelle or Liberty. Since thoughts of Liberty didn't cause him pain—only frustration—he allowed them to surface. Beyond her beauty, he'd sensed she had a good heart, that she was intelligent, caring. Something he'd been working hard to cultivate himself seemed to come naturally to her. Even without drinking of her, though, he'd come close to taking pleasure in her. Pleasure of a more sexual nature. She'd been his for the taking.

He snorted a laugh. But now she hated him. Just as well. The sooner she was gone, the sooner they could all get back to their normal lives. Or, now with Van Helsing gone, their abnormal lives… their doom.

His front door opened. He knew it was Ryan by his scent. Besides, not that many people would have the balls to enter without knocking. What was it with that stocky Aussie kid? More bravery than brains.

"So, no party tonight?"

"Sure. Party of one." Without turning around, Eli tipped the glass and drank.

"You can't do this. Can't close yourself off. We need your help."

"Help? There's no hope. No help."

Ryan slid on the stool next to him. "*She's* our hope. But you have to train her. Otherwise—"

"No way in hell am I training her. Have you seen her? Van Helsings are trained nearly from birth, so she's already eighteen years behind the curve. Victor chose to protect his little princess by sending her away. She doesn't stand a chance."

"With your help, she does."

Eli whirled to face him. "What part of 'get the hell

out of my face' do you not understand?" A growl left his throat. He extended his fangs, and his skin tightened on his face, his eyes burning.

Ryan flinched, but stood his ground. "You don't scare me, Eli. I'm not giving up until you agree. You're the only one who can give her the training she needs."

Eli breathed deeply and forced himself to relax. After a few seconds, the fangs retracted, and the flesh on his face eased, his eyes no longer burned.

"No one can give her the training she needs. Get it through your head. It's over. I thought when I—" He took a deep breath. "I thought once I got to know Van Helsing, we could make a difference. Now he's gone, and the only living person with Van Helsing blood is a dainty, whiny slip of a girl who has no idea how to hold a gun, let alone use one, or a bow, or a stake."

"But you have to try."

"I don't have to do anything right now except empty this bottle. Might as well accept it, we're doomed. The only way to handle that is to become numb." He downed the liquid and refilled the glass, holding the half empty bottle up to the light. Nice. Half way to his goal. Not bad. Not bad at all.

****

The funeral was held at dusk. No doubt so the vampires could attend. Equal opportunity and all. Liberty was so distraught over her father, that she couldn't feel frightened at the thought of vampires being in the crowd. After all, she didn't know which ones were which, so she pretended they were all humans. Except Eli. Him, she ignored.

Ryan had stayed by her side during the entire funeral, but she'd asked him for a moment alone with her father. Now, she stood at the graveside long after the service had ended and wiped tears off her cheeks. How could the grief be so deep for a man she barely knew? Her mind went to the photos they'd perused together. Happy times. Lots of happy times. She knew him. She might not remember knowing him, but he was her father, and she knew him. Now, she'd lost him. She held tightly onto Ryan's coin, letting its warmth soothe her. If there was ever a time in her life she needed to feel grounded, alive, it was now.

"Excuse me, miss?" She looked up. A man stood next to her. He was middle-aged, wearing a dark @grey suit. His hair was almost the same shade of grey, but on him, it looked distinguished, handsome. His blue eyes glittered in the semi-darkness. "You don't look familiar. Are you from here?"

"I've only been here a little more than a week."

"How well did you know Victor? I can't help but notice, you're quite broken up."

She sniffed back tears. "He—he was my fa—"

"Her father's friend." A voice behind her spoke, and she turned to find Eli standing a few feet away.

"Eli." The man gave a strained smile. "You look well."

"What are you doing here?"

"Paying my respects. Things won't be the same around here without a Van Helsing."

Eli's eyes narrowed. "I couldn't agree more."

Eli took Liberty's arm, and she resisted the urge to pull away, not wanting to make a scene. She gritted her teeth and tolerated his touch.

"If you'll excuse us," Eli said to the stranger.

"Certainly." The man looked at Liberty. "I'm sorry

for your loss. I hope to see more of you around the island." His eyes dropped, and he lifted her friendship necklace in his fingers and studied it, then took his time placing it back to rest against her skin. She flinched at the familiarity of his touch. "A lovely piece to hang around a lovely…" His eyes bore into Eli's. "…neck."

Liberty shivered, shooting a look at Eli. Was this man a vampire? Eli's mouth tightened. "Excuse us."

"Who was he?" she asked as Eli led her away, moving so quickly she almost had to run to keep up.

"His name is Rupert."

"Why didn't you want him to know Victor was my father?"

He halted abruptly and tightened his grip, staring down into her face. "You can't let anyone know that, got it? Word will get around soon enough, but the longer it takes, the better. You'll be a target."

"Not if you train me."

Where had that come from? When had she decided she wanted to fulfill her destiny? Let alone, try to convince Eli to help make it happen. If she were honest, it had been in the back of her mind since she'd learned the truth. Now, it had moved to the front.

He smirked. "You have to have at least a basis of strength, toughness, cunning, speed. You have none of that."

"You might be surprised."

"Then again, I might not." He released his hold. "See you around." He turned and strode away without another word.

****

Jerome had given her a few days off work, but she wished he hadn't. She had nothing to do but wander around the large, empty house, and listen to Antoine harp on the necessity of her fulfilling her destiny. He didn't, however, want her trained by anyone other than Eli. So, they were at an impasse.

Ryan came by to see her two days after the funeral. They sat next to one another on the sofa in the library.

"How are you?" His brown eyes squinted, but his mouth wasn't smiling. He gripped her hand in both of his, rubbing his fingers along her knuckles. "I've been worried about you."

Electricity moved over her skin, into her bloodstream. "I'm okay." She drew in a breath and gave a shaky laugh. "Actually, I'm totally bummed. Really, really sad. It's funny. I feel like I don't even have the right to grieve. I barely knew him."

Ryan smiled and stroked her cheek with his fingers. "Then maybe that's what you're grieving for."

Tears swam in her vision. She wiped them away and nodded. "Maybe so. Thanks."

"Any time."

"How are things at the bar?"

"Busy. Hectic." He smiled again. "Lonely without you."

She smiled back, feeling better than she had since her father's death—and since she'd learned about vampires. Her mind had rolled over everything she'd seen and heard the past few days. All she came up with were more questions.

"Did you ever find out who killed the girl at the party?"

Ryan shrugged. "Someone saw Kadin in the trees nearby a few minutes before it happened. Probably him."

"Kadin?"

"He's an EO. One of the worst. He enjoys his… tasks a little too much."

"What's the deal with Nadia and Diego? They don't like me. Are they vampires or just rude?"

"Diego is a vampire. Nadia isn't. They distrust outsiders. But I promise, when Diego finds out you're a Van Helsing, he'll change his attitude toward you. Can't make any promises about Nadia." He stood. "I'd better get to work. You'll be back tomorrow night?"

She nodded. "I'm actually looking forward to it. Help take my mind off of things." She hadn't decided yet if she'd stay. On one hand, her father was gone, and she missed her mother. She was equal parts tempted and frightened to become a vampire hunter. But if Eli wouldn't train her, what was the point? She should probably put all this behind her and go back home.

Home. Funny how the word seemed almost foreign to her. She'd changed since she arrived at Sang Croc. Would home even be the same now?

"I'm not scheduled tomorrow, but if you want, we could hang out after you get off. Maybe on the beach. Dinner and drinks. How does that sound?"

She smiled. She didn't have to make a decision about her plans, her future, right now. "That sounds awesome."

****

She got to work early and called her mother from the break room while waiting for her shift to start.

"Liberty, sweetie. I miss you so much. When are you coming home?"

Liberty squeezed her eyes shut against the longing that swept through her. "I miss you too, Mom." She sniffed back tears. "I don't know when I'll be back. I feel

80

like I should stay."

"What for? This man, whoever he was, is dead. There's nothing for you there."

Liberty wasn't sure how to handle this topic. It was crazy weird that her mother recalled nothing about her father, yet Liberty knew the whole truth. She decided to stick with vagueness. "I believe he was my father. That's what matters. Regardless, I grew close to him in the short time I knew him. And I've met a lot of great people here. The island is beautiful. I think I'll stay at least for a while."

"I don't understand why you'd even think about staying. Why you believe he was your father. Please just come home."

She couldn't have this conversation right now. There was no explanation that would satisfy, at least, none that she could give. "I love you, Mom. I have to go. My shift's starting."

She hung up and clocked in. Hannah and her grandparents were there again. She hadn't seen them in a while. Strangely, she'd missed them too. Not as bad as her friends and family, but she'd missed them a little. Chatting with Hanna lifted Liberty's spirits. She'd always wanted a little sister. Hannah almost seemed to hero worship her, and with the way Liberty had been feeling lately, it was kind of nice.

Although she hadn't worked in days, she found herself watching the clock inch away the hours. She'd be so glad when the shift ended. Mainly because of her date with Ryan. He was sweet… thoughtful… he made her feel less afraid. And he was so… hot.

She started her side work before the last of her customers left so she'd have a jump on it. Bianca was closing tonight, so Liberty would be the first cut.

She was filling ketchup bottles—the last chore on her list other than cleaning the tables. She peeked into the dining room. Damn. Still there. *Hurry, hurry, hurry. Just go already.* She hated it when she had squatters.

Bianca came up beside her to bring a few more empty ketchup bottles. The girl groaned, and Liberty looked up at her. Her face was pale, and she clutched her stomach.

"What's the matter?"

"Oh God, I don't know, but I feel like shit. I've thrown up three times in the last hour."

"Are you… well, you know." Liberty glanced around to make sure she wasn't overhead. She and Bianca had become fairly close, but she had no idea if Bianca was in a serious relationship. Or, if she slept around. She was twenty-one and gorgeous—not likely a virgin.

"No, I'm not pregnant," Bianca murmured. "I think I have a virus." She looked up at the clock on the wall and groaned again. "Three more hours. I'll never make it."

"I'll close for you." As soon as the words were out of Liberty's mouth, she regretted it. She was always doing that, speaking too soon and wishing she hadn't.

"Would you?" Bianca's expression showed such relief, Liberty felt bad about her less than generous thoughts.

"Sure. Go home and get some rest."

"Thank you. I'd give you a big fat kiss, but you might catch whatever I have. You're great, though. No wonder my brother's over the top for you."

"Over the top?"

She smiled. "He gave you our father's coin, right?"

"But… he said it was just a coin. Not *the* coin."

"Of course he did. He doesn't want *you* to know how over the top he is. Was from the second he saw you."

Liberty thought about Bianca's words for the rest of the night. Did Ryan really like her that much? In all the time she'd been with Cam, he'd never done anything as thoughtful as Ryan had the first time they met. She liked Ryan. But that much? She didn't think so. She was, however, looking forward to their date even more now that she knew how he felt. Although it would be a while before she could leave. In volunteering to cover Bianca, Liberty was stuck with Bianca's side work. And closing duties. And three more hours of work.

During a lull, she sent him a quick text letting him know she'd be later than they thought.

After closing, she had another table that lingered. She told Nadia, who was floor manager that night, to go home, and she'd lock up after the customers left. There was no need in both of them staying forever. Nadia agreed, but didn't say thank you. She hadn't shown even a glimmer of friendliness toward Liberty. Was it really only because Liberty was an outsider? The real question was, why did Liberty continue to be nice to her without reciprocation? Maybe her need to make friends was so strong she'd allow people to walk all over her. No matter. She couldn't change who she was. Nor could she change Nadia.

Liberty took extra care with the side work that night. Maybe it would help her get back in Jerome's good graces. She needed something other than intimidation by Eli, especially since she couldn't count on his assistance any longer.

The last customers finally left, and she took her cell from her purse to text Ryan. Hopefully it wasn't too late for them to hang out. That would totally suck.

She was typing the text when a scraping noise from the dining room caught her attention. Was someone in the restaurant? She'd locked the door, she was sure of it.

Heart pounding, she cautiously made her way into the dining room. She halted, drawing in a quick breath when she saw a man standing in the center of the room, resting his hands on the back of a chair, as if waiting for her.

He was tall with white-blond hair and some kind of tattoo along his jaw bone. She shivered. *Creepy looking.*

Forcing the fear from her voice, she said, "I'm sorry. We're closed." How had he gotten in? She was sure she'd locked the door. Unless he was a…

Her eyes flew to his face. He grinned and sauntered toward her. She backed up until she was pressed against the wall behind the bar. It was then she remembered she still held her cell. She punched the button to call… Antoine? What help would he be? Ryan would just get himself hurt… or killed. Eli… out of the question.

The man continued to move slowly and steadily toward her.

Oh God… was 9-1-1 the same number on the island? Why hadn't she ever thought to ask?

Chapter 7

He lunged forward so fast he became just a blur, and he was on her, gripping her throat, his fingers like steel. Her cell phone flew from her hands and clattered to the floor. He pulled her toward him, their faces only centimeters apart. His eyes flickered, then turned a fiery red. He opened his mouth in a grotesque smile, fangs protruding—just like Eli's had. She whimpered, trying to pull away, but couldn't budge his grip.

"I got you now." His fetid breath, like something from the grave, wafted over her. "He wants me to bring you back alive, but no reason I can't have a little fun before taking you."

"Who—who wants you to—" Before she could finish the sentence, he flicked his hand as if brushing away an insect, and she flew into the mirrored wall. Glass broke, shattering over her head and onto her face. Sharp pain pierced her cheeks, her shoulder, followed by wet stickiness.

Blood. She was bleeding… oh God. Before she had time to worry about the blood, he latched onto her neck, lifted her, with her feet dangling above the ground. She couldn't breathe… agony shot through her neck, up to her jaw, her head. She clawed at his hands where they gripped—*held her in the air* by her throat… Tears sprang to her eyes, but her circulation to her brain was cut off, and they hovered there, paralyzed by pain.

"What do you want?" Air squeezed out of her chest, pain and fear making her words barely a whimper.

"If there wasn't a chance you were a Van Helsing, I'd drink you dry." He growled and opened his mouth, giving her an up close and personal view of the fangs.

Think, think, think. Terror seized her brain. Should she admit she was a Van Helsing? How would that prevent him from biting her… tasting her blood? Bile rose to her chest. This could not be happening. Spots danced in front of her eyes. Her head swam with dizziness. She was going to pass out, and this monster would…

The dizziness increased, and the spots merged, becoming a black blanket. Good, maybe if she passed out, the pain would stop, and she could forget about the blood dripping from her face—*her* blood. Nausea seized her stomach. If she lost consciousness, what would he do to her while she was out?

Before another thought could take hold, the pressure eased, and she was free. She fell to the ground in a heap. Confused, she squinted upward. Eli?

He had the vampire by the throat. He tossed him across the room as easily as he would hurl a Frisbee. The vampire landed with a loud crash against the wall. Photos hanging above him smashed to the ground, some landing on his head then bouncing to the floor next to him. Jerome was going to be pissed.

She rose unsteadily to her feet and swayed. She couldn't run, couldn't help, could only stand in frozen silence, focused on the battle raging before her.

The vampire came off the floor in a flash, lunged at Eli, slamming his fist into Eli's face. Eli stumbled backward, then caught his bearings and elbowed the vampire in the chest just as he was moving in for another strike. The vampire flew back into the same wall, but recovered quickly and launched to his feet. He shoved Eli across the room, and Eli crash-landed into a wooden table, splintering it into pieces. Jerome was *really* going to be pissed.

Frantically, Liberty's gaze searched the bar. There had to be something to use as a weapon. She should help Eli. No matter what she thought of him, he had rescued her. This newcomer was definitely the scarier of the two.

Nothing. Not a single item she could use as a weapon.

Only certain things could stop a vampire, right? Holy water… none to be found… a cross would slow them down, but she didn't have one of those either. She silently berated herself for not being more religious. Garlic? In the kitchen, garlic. Wait, that only kept them away. It didn't hurt them. A stake. She needed a wooden stake. She'd have to talk to Jerome about stocking the bar with wooden stakes. Now that she thought about it, since he knew of the existence of vampires, why wouldn't he have already done that?

The thoughts tumbled on top of one another, occurring in no more than ten seconds. She grabbed the largest bottle of whiskey from behind the bar and headed toward the two men. Her legs shook so badly she could barely move, but she had to help. But what good would a glass bottle do?

The vampire was advancing on Eli—who lay perfectly, frighteningly still in the heap of table rubble.

He hadn't moved since he'd landed there. Was he unconscious… dead?

No, vampires didn't die that easily. The bottle might

not do any good, but she could at least offer a diversion. Maybe give Eli time to wake up.

The vampire swayed and took a step toward Eli.

"Hey," she shouted.

He looked over his shoulder at her, lurching like a drunk. "I'll deal with you in a minute—"

The words ended on a whoomf. His eyes widened. Blood spurted from his mouth. What the…?

She glanced downward. The pointed end of a table leg protruded from his chest. Her gaze moved past him to where Eli stood, panting heavily. The vampire dropped to the ground, his upper body bowed where the makeshift stake was speared to the floor. A sizzling sound was followed by a putrid burning smell, then the body just… burst into flames. After a few seconds, the corpse was a pile of dust. *God…* insane… All of this was so insane.

She looked up at Eli. "I—how did you…?" She brought up a shaking hand to brush her hair back. Blood was smeared all over her skin, her clothing. Deep, burning pain she hadn't noticed in her terror shot through her shoulder. She took an unsteady step toward Eli, then sank to the floor.

Only half conscious, she was vaguely aware of being lifted. Of strong arms holding her against a hard chest. Of cool skin through the black shirt he wore. Cold. So cold, but safe…

She linked her hands behind his neck. The night breeze kissed her skin as they left the tiki bar. Blackness shuttered over her eyes, and she knew no more.

****

Images came and went like photos in a slide show. Dr. Lemanu bent over her, peering into her eyes, saying she'd be okay, she'd wake soon. That was real, she thought. Then an image of Eli holding onto her hand, his eyes darkened to slate, whispering, "I'm sorry I didn't get there sooner. Please don't die on me."

Was that one real? It couldn't be. He'd shown such tenderness, such concern. Not at all like a monster.

Would a monster save your life?

Her eyes fluttered open and met Eli's. "Am I dreaming?" she whispered.

He grinned and opened his mouth to answer, but a sharp pain pierced her shoulder, and she cried out. No. Not dreaming. Dreams didn't hurt that bad.

"Hurts." Her voice was a croaked whisper. Her mouth felt like she'd eaten sand.

"Here, drink this." Eli put a straw to her lips, and she drank. Cool water coated her mouth and tongue. *Heavenly.*

"Thank you."

Eli said something, but she couldn't make out the words. His reply sounded far away. She felt herself floating, drifting into space.

She wasn't sure how much time passed before she tugged her lids open again. A lamp burned at her bedside, casting a dim glow. Voices rose to her consciousness.

"I'll kill him."

"You don't know it was Rupert."

Rupert? Where had she heard that name? Oh yeah, the man at the funeral.

"Who else? He suspects she's a Van Helsing. They won't stop."

Was that Eli? His smooth voice sounded ragged, exhausted.

He'd saved her. Why?

Ryan's face filled her vision. "Hey, you're awake, how do you feel?" He smiled, but worry clouded his brown eyes.

"I'm… sore. Okay, though." She looked past him where Eli stood, his brows drawn into a frown, his jaw tight. "Thanks to Eli. What were you doing there?"

"Antoine was worried. He asked me to check on you. What the hell were you doing there alone at that time of night?"

He moved next to Ryan and scowled down at her.

"I—was closing." She looked back up at Ryan. "Sorry I couldn't keep our date."

"Date?" Eli bit out the word.

Ryan quirked a brow. "Yeah, date. Dinner and drinks on the beach."

Eli turned on him, fists clenched at his sides. "When she didn't show up, you didn't go check on her?" Fury infused the words.

"I texted him and told him I had to close," Liberty said. "Bianca was sick, so I covered for her."

"That reminds me," Ryan said. "I need to let her know you're okay. She's been worried sick. Feels guilty."

"She shouldn't. She had no way of knowing."

Ryan smiled and moved away from the bed but stayed in the room. In a moment, she heard him talking to Bianca.

Eli turned to look down at her. His silvery eyes glinted like hard steel. He stroked his cool fingers along her cheek, sending a shiver over her flesh. "You almost died," he whispered.

She swallowed back a lump that rose to her throat and shook her head. "He said he couldn't kill me. He just wanted to…" The hiss of that hateful voice filled her ears. She drew in a deep breath. "Wanted to… have some fun before he took me to him."

"Him?" Eli's jaw tightened. "Who?"

"He didn't say."

Ryan had ended the call and moved back to her side. Eli whirled to face him. "Rupert. Now do you believe me?"

"Maybe. I wonder how he knew she'd be there alone. Do you think he's having her followed?"

"Could be."

Ryan let out a weary sigh. "Lot of good it does, even if we knew it was him. Without a Van Helsing to ward them off…" he trailed away.

Eli turned back to her. "You're leaving. Going back to Oklahoma on the next flight out. Next time, I might not be there."

Why did he want to protect her? Why was he looking at her with that soft yet fierce look in his eyes? Did he care more than he let on? The true question was, why did it matter? He was a vampire. She was a vampire hunter.

It struck her then. Her destiny. *I am a Vampire hunter.*

"I'm not leaving." Her voice was firm in spite of how weak she felt, in spite of her dry throat. "I'm a Van Helsing. I can't turn my back on that." She rose to sit against the headboard and spoke to Ryan, "Do you think Diego will train me?"

"Yeah." Ryan sighed. "He will. Not as well as you should be. But he'll do it."

"She'll never be an effective weapon against Rupert and his vamps." Eli scraped a hand through his hair.

"What's wrong with you people?"

"What's wrong with you?" Ryan's voice rose. "We have to at least try."

"For God's sake," Eli growled at Liberty. "If you're not smart enough to leave, I'll train you. At least then there'll be maybe a five percent chance you won't get yourself killed."

****

Liberty's legs burned, and her chest felt like it was going to burst. She stopped running and bent over at the waist, her hands on her knees.

"Why are you stopping?"

She shot a glare at Eli. "I can't—can't—" She puffed out breaths from her strained lungs. "I can't run anymore."

He crossed his arms. "You'll never get in shape if you can't work through the burn."

When she got her breath semi under control, she straightened. Strands of hair had escaped her ponytail and clung to her damp cheeks. She brushed them off her face. "I've done nothing but pushups, pull-ups, and running for four days. When am I going to actually learn to fight?"

"Have you ever actually fought?"

She shrugged. "Do pillow fights with my girlfriends count?"

He lifted a brow. "What were you wearing?"

"Wearing?" She frowned. "Why? Does it matter?"

He grinned. "Nah. That was just for me."

She crossed her arms and glowered, fighting the urge to grin back. When had her fear of him turned into this easy camaraderie? Maybe the night he'd saved her from a true monster? "Seriously. I want to learn something more than I'd learn in a gym class."

"You need to build up your stamina and your upper body strength."

"For how long? Geez."

He blew a breath out and rolled his eyes. "God, you're a pain in the ass. Fine. I'll mix in some weapon training along with it. Come on."

She followed him through the dark night and into his house, then to a back bedroom. This obviously wasn't his room. It was small, and the only furniture was a double bed, a chest of drawers, and built-in cabinets that covered one wall. It didn't feel lived in. Tight quarters forced her into close proximity to him. She pulled at her tank top, running her finger around the edge of the neckline. She must smell. She'd been sweating outside for the past two hours. It was a good thing she was no longer interested in him romantically.

He moved to the cabinets and flung two doors open. The space was filled to capacity with various weapons.

"Wow," she breathed.

Eli began pulling out items, shoving them into her arms, one at a time. Two pistols, a bow, a holder with arrows sticking out of it. She sagged under the weight. He rummaged around some more. Surely he wasn't looking for anything else. She could barely hold what he'd given her.

He pulled out an armful of sharp wooden sticks—stakes—along with a vest and added them to the pile. "Bullet proof vest. The vamps will have weapons."

"I don't need it now, though, right?"

"I want you to get used to moving in it. Running in it."

"You're not carrying anything?"

"If you can't carry them, you can't use them."

He left the room, and she followed, adjusting the weapons in her arms to try to keep from dropping them.

They walked behind his house—a ways behind his house—until he finally stopped. He took the weapons from her and laid them on the ground.

"We'll start with the bow." He picked it up. "In ancient times, only those of high rank participated in archery." He lifted the holder with the arrows. "This is a quiver," he said, slinging the strap onto her back. She staggered under the sudden weight. "Back then, although those who trained were excellent marksmen, the bow wasn't used in war. Archery was a sacred sport." He took the bow from her, pulled an arrow out of the quiver, strung it, and let it fly. The yard was lit up well enough for her to see that it landed dead center in the trunk of a palm tree more than forty yards away. He looked at her over his shoulder and grinned. "We, however, don't share their reverence."

"So, you think you can teach me to do that?"

"Not a chance."

She scowled. He could at least *pretend* he thought she might get good at this.

"Here, hold this." He handed her the bow. "And don't shoot me." He winked. "Just kidding. You couldn't hit me if I stood right in front of you."

He missed her sticking her tongue out at him when he turned and jogged about five yards ahead to where a low table sat. He bent and picked up cans from the ground, lining them up along the table, then ran back to her.

"Okay. You're right handed, correct?" She nodded. "Then your left hand is your bow hand, your right hand your draw hand." He pointed to the hard plastic of the bow. "These are the limbs. This handle here in the center is the riser."

"Okay. That's easy enough."

"This is anything but easy. Just pay attention, okay?"

"Fine," she muttered.

"You'll need to figure out your anchor point. Most people use their cheekbone. This is the place where you'll rest your draw hand each time. Once you decide on a spot, you need to stick with it. You'll have to practice a lot, figure out your own shooting instinct by seeing where the arrow goes and adjusting accordingly."

"I will. I promise."

He handed her the bow. "Now. When you load an arrow, it's called nocking. The slot in the bottom is the nock, and when you put the string in the slot, you're nocking the arrow, got it?" She nodded again. "You're going to draw the bow, which means pull back on the arrow and string at the same time. This is when you'll need to find your anchor point. Wherever your index and middle fingers touch, use the same spot each time, it keeps your release consistent."

"Got it." The bow felt foreign in her hands… dangerous. Yet it oddly filled her with a sense of power. But could she ever actually use it on another person— even a vampire? She'd better be able to. The time would come when she might not have a choice.

"Now, pull back. Aim at the cans. Take in a breath, let it out slowly. When the breath is about halfway out, you release the arrow and the string simultaneously. Ready?"

"Ready."

"Let's see what you got."

She did as instructed.

When she released the arrow, the string snapped her left wrist, stinging like she'd been bull whipped, and the arrow landed ineffectually a foot or so on the ground in front of her.

"Ow!" She dropped the bow and rubbed her wrist where a red welt had already appeared.

He picked the bow up and thrust it at her. "Go again."

"That hurt."

"You'll get over it. Let's go." He moved behind her and reached his arms around to grip the bow. "Don't lock your left elbow. That's how you get hurt."

She pursed her lips in irritation. "That would have been nice to know beforehand."

"You'll remember things better if you make mistakes."

He was so close, his words vibrated over her skin. She suppressed a shiver, nearly forgetting about the pain in her wrist. He wrapped his hands around her fingers and pressed them against the riser. Something warm and pleasant spread through her belly. She swallowed against the sudden dryness in her throat. How could a vampire, with a cold body, cause such heat to rush through her?

"Focus," he said into her ear. "With your left hand, you have to push away from yourself and with your right hand you pull, you don't lock in position, it's a continual movement."

Her heart pounded so hard, she couldn't speak, so she nodded.

Still holding her hand, he pulled the string back. "Hold your breath."

She didn't tell him that wasn't a problem since it was locked inside her throat.

"Now, keep your left elbow loose and halfway through the breath, release."

She let go, and the arrow shot straight forward, missing the cans by no more than half a foot.

"Yes!" she squealed. She turned in his arms. "I did it!" Her movements brought her face close to his. His eyes looked into hers, the silver rimmed in sapphire.

Silence hung between them. The only sound was the distant waves lapping against the shore and Liberty's breaths whistling in and out of her lungs. He cleared his throat and stepped back. "Yeah. You did it. Let's go again."

For the next hour, they practiced with the bow, then switched to the pistol. She hit fifty percent of the targets, which was a vast improvement from her initial zero percent.

She pulled her phone out of her sweat pants pocket to check the time. "Geez. It's two a.m." She yawned. "I'm exhausted, and you're not even winded."

He shrugged. "One of the advantages of being a vampire. Come on, let's keep going."

Chapter 8

Rupert Kilbourne paced the length of his library. In a few hours, it would be daylight. But before that time came, he would feed. If the fools would hurry up and bring the girl to him. He poured scotch from a decanter and downed the liquid. It burned from his throat into his stomach, but didn't satisfy his hunger. Only one thing would do that. Where were the imbeciles?

Finally, the door opened. Two of his men held the girl, one on each arm as she struggled against them, sobbing and kicking. Rupert smiled. He liked them feisty. He could mesmerize her—sometimes, he did— but tonight, he was in the mood for a challenge.

The men tossed her to the floor in front of him. She scrambled to her feet, poised to flee, but he flicked out a hand and snatched her up by her hair.

"You may go." He spoke to his men but kept his gaze focused on the woman. In seconds, the door clicked shut.

"Please," the girl cried. "Please let me go."

Rupert smiled. "Not quite yet." *Maybe not at all.*

He held the young blonde's hair, tugging her head back until the vein in her neck stood out in the soft flesh of her neck. She whimpered and pushed against his chest, her efforts as ineffectual as that of a fly against a whirlwind.

"Shhh," he whispered.

But she didn't listen. They never did. Her cries grew louder. She shouted for help.

"Sorry, my dear. No one will come to your aid."

He smiled, then extended his fangs and sank them into her skin. She let out a guttural scream. Warm, sweet blood pulsed into his mouth. He groaned, drinking in the elixir. This was the moment he always had a decision to make. Drink just enough to satisfy his hunger, or keep taking until he emptied her veins, until the life ebbed from her body?

Normally, he practiced restraint, but tonight, he felt reckless. The new girl had him turned inside out. Was she just a friend of Victor's or did she have Van Helsing blood pulsing through her veins?

He had to know. Had to own her. Once he did, once he determined if she was a Van Helsing, he would take action. If she was, he would use her blood to his advantage. Not drinking from her, of course, he wasn't suicidal. But he would siphon it from her body, store it for its healing powers. For the humans in his fold who were victims of a too enthusiastic vampire. Or, for punishment of the vampires who dared defy him, those who screwed up as Kadin had when Rupert sent him to retrieve her. Instead of following his instructions to the letter, Kadin had decided to toy with her. In doing so, he'd lost his life and given Eli an opportunity to come to her rescue. Who knew Eli would set himself up as a hero?

In spite of himself, a fissure of pride wound through him. Eli was full of surprises. A strong and capable warrior. But he was also foolish. Too often ruled by his emotions.

Emotions were detrimental to a vampire. That's

why, when he'd drained the last ounce of blood from the blonde, when he dropped the empty husk that had once been a body to the floor where it landed with a hollow thud, he felt nothing but detached satisfaction.

****

The night following her training session, Liberty nervously applied make-up and smoothed the skirt of her green silk dress. Ryan had invited her to an annual festival, Heiva. Both Jerome and Eli had given her the night off, and she was not only relieved to get a respite from the training, she was relieved to have an evening away from Eli. Being around him caused this odd combination of fear and desire, and it was screwing with her head.

Ryan had told her to wear something pretty. She hoped he'd approve. She had never gone out with a guy other than Cam, and she was a bundle of nerves.

When she reached the bottom of the stairs, the doorbell rang. Antoine was nowhere in sight, so Liberty opened it. Ryan stood on the porch. He wore shiny gray pants and a matching jacket over a white shirt with the first few buttons undone. One word came to mind… *hot*.

"Wow." His smile made his eyes dance. "You look amazing."

"Thanks. So do you."

"You ready?" He offered his arm, and she took it and let him lead her to the car.

They drove to the beach and parked, then walked across the sand to a row of tables lined along the water. "Milady." Ryan bowed and swept a hand out toward a chair.

She laughed and took a seat. "I never knew you had such a flair for the dramatic."

"Yeah?" He bent low and whispered in her ear. "Tonight might hold all kinds of surprises."

Her breath caught in her throat, and her eyes latched onto his mouth. He leaned in, and she waited for his lips to touch hers. Waited for their first kiss. Excitement tingled through her as he slowly, excruciatingly inched closer.

"Ah, there you are."

Liberty jerked at the sound of Eli's voice. Damn him!

Ryan straightened and faced Eli who strode toward them. He wore jeans with a black button up shirt and a silver tie that matched his eyes. His normally mussed hair was neatly combed. "I haven't missed the fire dancers yet, have I?"

"What are you doing here?" Ryan gritted his teeth.

"Out to enjoy the festivities, just like you." Eli dropped into a chair and looked up at Ryan. "Pull up a chair, my man. No need to stand."

Liberty leaned her elbows on the table and glared at him. "This is a date."

"Shhhh." He pointed over her shoulder. "Show's about to start."

Ryan grabbed a chair from a nearby table and planted it close to Liberty, then sat.

The sounds of drumming filled the air. In the center of the beach, a native man wearing nothing but a thin cloth over his groin held a flaming torch in each hand. He began to move his body with the music, at the same time, twirling the torches.

"He's not wearing any clothes," Liberty whispered, awed by the sight.

Eli leaned close and murmured, "With all that fire

flying around, would you?"

She didn't answer; her gaze was locked on the display before her. The man spun the torches so fast, they looked like unbroken circles of fire glowing in the night.

More dancers joined him after the first song, and Liberty soon forgot there were strange naked men dancing on the sand. The show was breathtaking. She was barely aware of the dinner a Polynesian woman placed in front of her. Barely able to taste the food as she watched in rapt attention. The one thing she couldn't ignore was Eli sitting across the table from her. But when Ryan scooted his chair closer and took her hand, she was almost able to forget Eli was there.

"Wow." She shook her head when the show ended. "That was… phenomenal."

"Pretty awesome, huh?" Ryan said. "I've seen so many shows, I'd almost forgotten how amazing it was. Until I saw it through your eyes."

"Aw, isn't that sweet. You two make the cutest couple."

Ryan glared at Eli. "What the hell are you doing here? She has the night off, you know."

"There's a full moon in two weeks. Even a night off can't really be a night off."

"Full moon?" Liberty knew vampires had to turn a human on a full moon, but she wasn't sure what that had to do with her… or her training.

"Yeah. We left out the fun part." Eli's mouth tightened into a grimacing smile. "That's the night you hunt."

Liberty shot her gaze to Ryan. "Is he serious? I have to hunt vampires?"

Eli snorted a laugh. "What did you think vampire

hunter was, a cutesie nickname?"

She ignored his sarcasm. "I knew I had to defend against them, if the situation presented itself. But hunt?"

Ryan moved his chair closer and took both her hands in his. "I won't let anything happen to you."

Eli leaned across the table. "How do you plan to prevent it inside your closed and locked doors?"

Ryan spoke without taking his eyes off Liberty. "I won't be inside. I'm going with her."

"The hell you are," Eli growled.

"What's going on?" Liberty asked. "Why can't he?"

"Because." Eli clenched his jaw as he spoke. "The full moon is when the EO's come out in droves. They're hunting for people to turn. As Ryan told you before, the locals know to stay inside. *Ryan* knows to stay inside."

"I'm going with Liberty."

Eli stood and grabbed Ryan by the shirt collar and jerked him to his feet, pulling him away from Liberty. "Do you want to become a vampire? Huh? No? I didn't think so. You'll stay inside. That's the end of it."

Ryan tugged away and straightened his shirt. He knelt in the sand next to Liberty's chair. "I'll be there."

"No, you won't." Tears clogged her voice, and she swallowed them back. She was terrified to face the vampires, but she was more terrified for Ryan to. "You can't take that chance. I'll be fine. I've learned a lot."

"And you know they won't bite her," Eli said. "They'll have to use weapons, and she'll be wearing protection."

"Why won't they bite me?"

"Legend has it that a Van Helsing's blood is fatal to a vampire. But not just that it kills them. It drives them insane, sometimes makes them self-mutilate. One story is that a vampire tore his own face off after drinking from a Van Helsing."

"Oh God." Waves of nausea rose and shifted in her stomach. The dinner she'd eaten earlier threatened to surface. The images, the violence of this culture, were just too horrific. She looked up at Eli. "You'll be there, though, right?"

He dropped his gaze. "Right. I'll be there."

If that were true, then why wouldn't he look at her?

****

Liberty met Eli for training after getting off of a nine hour shift. The full moon was less than a week away. She couldn't slow down. But God, was she exhausted. She was getting better, though. Stronger. More confident. More skilled with the weapons. She was actually starting to think she might not get herself killed her first night out. Maybe.

"So, what's the deal with Rupert?" she asked Eli as they took target practice, switching from pistols, to bows, back to pistols. She was now hitting targets ten yards out with the bow. Eli said that was exceptional progress. His praise filled her with warmth, but she didn't let him know.

"Rupert?"

"I heard you and Ryan talking about him. The man I met at my dad's funeral. You think he was behind my attack?"

"He's behind pretty much everything the EO's do. He's their leader."

"And he's free to move about in public? Like at the funeral? Why don't you just kill him?"

"Can't."

"Why not?"

"He mesmerized someone in town. Won't tell us who it is, but if Rupert is killed, that person has been told to kill their family, then take their own life."

Her blood froze. He was truly evil.

"Will he be… out? The night of the full moon? Will I run into him?"

Eli shrugged. "Not likely. He does his feeding mostly inside the fortress of his house. His minions often bring him his victims. But," His eyes lifted to hers. "He's taken a special interest in you. He might venture out just for that reason."

And she would have to battle him, without killing him, even if she knew how?

Eli smiled and lifted his hand, running it gently down her cheek. "Don't worry. You'll be fine. You've got the best trainer known to hunters. It's not often a hunter is trained by an actual vampire. It definitely gives you an edge. I know how we think."

She smiled back. "Thanks." She bit her lip, the words that had been on the tip of her tongue for weeks straining to get out. "Eli, I wanted to tell you… I'm sorry I was rude to you. In the beginning. When I found out. You can't help what—who you are. You're not a bad person. You saved me."

He shrugged. "Don't read too much into it. It was instinct."

"It was more than that. I saw the worry in your face. The relief when you realized I'd be okay. You risked your life for me."

He cupped her face in his hands, staring into her eyes. "Don't look at me like I'm a hero. I'm anything but."

You're my hero. The words almost left her mouth.

WTF? She must be exhausted. What was she thinking? She tugged away and stepped back. "I never said you were a hero. Let's get back to work."

God. What was wrong with her? She liked Ryan, she really did. A lot. But sometimes, when she was around Eli, she almost forgot about Ryan. Eli was all that mattered in those moments. And that was as dangerous as hunting vampires.

****

Eli fought back sympathy when Liberty grimaced. They'd been at it for hours. And before she'd started training tonight, she'd worked her ass off waiting tables. She needed to quit that damn job.

Exhaustion tugged down the corners of her lovely mouth. Her evergreen eyes were ringed with dark circles. He clamped his jaw tight and closed his non-living heart to the pain and fatigue in her face. If she didn't toughen up, she'd die. So would a lot of other people. Now that he'd committed, he was in it all the way. He couldn't show weakness… compassion. No matter how fragile her pale skin and weary smile made her seem.

He pushed her harder than he had any other night. They worked until just before sun up. This time, he carried the weapons back to the house. She plodded behind him, staggering once and almost falling to her knees. He shot out a free hand to steady her.

After storing the weapons in the cabinet, he led her to his car. She dropped into the soft cushioned seat and leaned her head back, brushing damp, tangled hair from her face. "So tired," she said around a yawn.

He'd barely pulled out of his drive before she was sound asleep.

At the Van Helsing house, he climbed out and

opened the passenger door. Sliding one arm beneath her knees and one behind her back, he gently lifted her from the car. Her head lolled against his shoulder. His chest tightened at the soft feel of her against him. He tilted his head, the urge to rub his cheek along the silky hair more powerful than any craving for blood he'd ever had. He gritted his teeth and forced the thought away. *Get a grip, man. She's not for you. Not in a million years.*

Favreau opened the door as soon as Eli stepped onto the porch. He moved back and gestured for Eli to enter, then followed him up the stairs.

Antoine turned the knob to her bedroom, and Eli went inside and lowered her onto the mattress. She didn't move. Her thick lashes cast a shadow against her pale cheeks. Her breasts rose and fell with her steady breathing. That same tightening came back to his chest, moving up to his throat.

"I can take it from here," Antoine said. "How did she do?"

Eli curled his lip. "She's getting better," he whispered. "But she's not a warrior."

"She must learn to be." Antoine put a hand on Eli's arm, and he turned to face the older man. "She cannot be your *Grande Amour.*"

"I know that," he snapped, still whispering.

"Does she?"

"She is with Ryan."

"A woman, especially a young woman her age, can have many loves. Does she know why she can never be yours?"

A whoosh of air escaped Eli's lungs. He didn't want to discuss this with Antoine—or anyone else for that matter. He knew Liberty had to mate with a human. She had to continue the Van Helsing line… have babies with another man. He couldn't give her that. Not ever. He damn sure didn't need Antoine reminding him.

He shook his head, then spun and stalked from the room.

Chapter 9

The full moon was two days away. Liberty couldn't believe she'd actually be fighting vampires. Only a month ago, she was graduating from high school, and now she was on an island eons from her home, learning how to kill vampires. Could she do it? When it came down to it, could she actually kill someone? She was a Van Helsing in name, but in her heart, she was just a scared Okie girl.

This was the last night of training before the battle. Eli wanted her to take the night off tomorrow. Rest and get her mind straight. But what kind of mindset would she have to be in to really be prepared?

"Okay, you ready?" Eli crossed his arms and lifted a brow.

"Ready for what?"

"No weapons tonight. You've had enough practice on them for the time being. Tonight, it's hand to hand combat."

"With you?"

He shrugged. "I'm your trainer. Who else?"

She took a deep breath and nodded. "I'm ready."

They circled one another. Liberty kept her eyes locked on his face. Eli had taught her to sense an opponent's move by the expressions on their face. When they were about to move in, their eyes would reveal their intentions.

She saw his flicker just before he lunged. She whirled, turning her back to him. She sensed him reach for her and grabbed his bicep, wrapping both hands around it. Bending at the waist, she summoned all her strength and rolled him over her back, then flipped him. He grunted when he hit the ground. She sprang on top of him, straddled his chest with her knees and clutched his throat. Triumphant, she smiled down at him.

They were both breathing heavily. He brought his hands up and wrapped them around her wrist. "Okay, I give," he choked.

She released him and rested her hands on her thighs. "See, I told you I—"

Without warning, he bucked and unseated her. She flailed backward and in the next moment was lying on the cool, damp grass looking up at him. He now straddled her. His hand lightly gripped her neck.

"What the hell?" she sputtered. "I thought it was over."

"Lesson one. Never trust an enemy is defeated, no matter what they say. Fight to the death."

"Okay. Fine. Now get off me." She squirmed beneath him.

His jaw tightened, and his breaths became shallow. His eyes glittered, moving down to her mouth. The hand on her neck gentled, stroked her skin. Heat simmered in her mid section where their bodies touched. He leaned forward, his lips coming closer to hers, his eyes searching her face. Above them, the blackness of the sky was broken by a smattering of tiny, diamond-like stars. The nearly full moon hovered like a warning sign. But all she could think about, all she could focus on, was Eli, how close he was... how he made her heart stutter in her chest. She was frozen, immobilized by the rush of unexpected desire. She wanted him to kiss her. Wanted to feel his firm lips against hers.

Ryan. Remember him?

She closed her eyes and willed the yearning away. "Get off me," she bit out.

Eli's hand tensed momentarily on her throat, then he growled and in seconds, coolness replaced the warmth as his body left hers.

She looked up at him. He stood, holding a hand out to her, still breathing heavily. She took his hand, and he helped her to her feet.

"You did well." His voice sounded strained.

"Do you think I'm ready?"

He let out a short bark. "As ready as you'll ever be."

She nodded and brushed her hands off on the seat of her sweat pants. "So, how does this work? What's the plan? How do I find the EO's? How do I tell them apart from the other vampires?"

"The plan is for you to go into town that night. Only a few businesses—vampire owned businesses—will be open. Tourists will be out, but not in their usual masses, partly due to their wish to honor the 'tradition' of the islanders to stay inside during full moons, and partly because there isn't that much to do with so many places closed. The EO's will be out, but they won't make themselves all that obvious. They practice a little discretion in fear of running off tourists. Of eliminating their food source—not to mention their pool of potential vampires. You'll watch, and wait. If you get the opportunity—*when* you get the opportunity, you'll take down as many vampires as you can."

"How will I be able to tell the vampires from the

humans?"

A cocky grin appeared. "They'll be the ones with their fangs in someone's neck."

She twisted her mouth. "Very funny. What about telling the bad ones from the good?"

He shrugged. "That's a little trickier. We'll be feeding that night too. Out to turn someone. We're supposed to keep a low profile. Turn one person, and only one person, and do so in the privacy of our homes, a hotel, somewhere like that. We shouldn't be out in the open, exposed. Not everyone follows that guideline."

"And if they don't, I could kill a good vampire."

Another shrug. "Yeah. That's a chance you'll have to take. Look at it this way, if they're not being… cautious, then at least you're ridding the world of a stupid vampire."

"Ah. That's a comfort." She rolled her eyes. "How does it feel? When you turn someone?"

His eyes narrowed. He was silent for several seconds, his jaw clenched. Finally, he said, "Like power and pain, all at the same time. Especially when I turn someone who doesn't want to be a vampire."

"Who *would* want to be? I mean, who have you turned who wanted to become a vampire?"

"A lot of people. Diego, for one."

"Why did he want to turn?"

Eli started back to the house, and she fell into step beside him. "His old man is an asshole. Used to beat the crap out of Diego, his mom, and his little sister. Diego figured the only way he could stop it was to turn."

"And?"

Eli grinned in the darkness. "His old man is terrified of him now. Hasn't laid a hand on any of them in three years."

Inside the house, she gathered her bag. "So you more or less do charity work?"

"I do what I have to do. Period."

She nodded and headed to the door. "And I guess that's what I'll do. Whatever I have to."

"I hope so. Otherwise, you die."

****

Eli drove Liberty home. She was about to get out of the car, when she noticed a figure on her porch. Fear gripped her chest. Who would be at her house in the middle of the night? Fear turned to worry when she recognized Hannah.

"Who is that?" Eli asked.

"A girl I met at Perfect Getaway."

"What's she doing here?"

"I have no idea, but I'm about to find out."

"Want me to come with you?"

"No. I can handle this. Thanks, though."

She climbed from the car and rushed up to the porch. "Hannah? What are you doing here? Is everything okay?"

The girl nodded. "I snuck out of the hotel."

"Why?"

"My grandparents are so overprotective. I wanted to have some fun."

"You shouldn't be out this time of night by yourself. Where have you been?"

"I went to a bar."

It was then Liberty noticed she was slurring her words. She swayed on her feet.

"They let you into a bar? Served you alcohol?"

She giggled and nodded emphatically. "I guess I

look older than I am."

God. A wasted thirteen-year-old. Just what she needed.

"Why did you come here?"

She lifted her shoulders and let them drop. "I didn't want to go back yet. My grandparents will kill me."

Liberty had no idea how the girl knew where she lived, but word traveled quickly on the island, and everyone knew where the Van Helsing house was. It wouldn't be hard to track her down.

She took Hannah gently by the arm. "Let's get you inside. Into bed. I'll call your grandparents in the morning."

When Liberty reached for the door, the whoosh of flapping wings sounded. She whirled to see a large bat heading straight toward them. She threw her arm around Hannah's shoulder and yanked her to the ground, crouching over her. A horrendous squeaking, rubbery noise pierced the still night.

Liberty looked up to see that, instead of a bat, a man—a vampire—stood on the porch. He was stocky with pale skin and short dark hair. His eyes gleamed red, his face a gray, cracked mask. Before she could react, he lunged for Hannah and snatched her right out of Liberty's arms. Hannah screamed. The creature grabbed a handful of hair and tilted her head back. Liberty watched in stunned horror as he sank his fangs into her neck.

"No!" Liberty lunged to her feet and launched on the vampire's back, pounding her fists against his head and shoulders. He didn't budge. Why the hell didn't she have a weapon? What good was it to learn to use them if she didn't carry one with her?

Sobbing and screaming, terror squeezing her heart, she struggled to free Hannah from the vampire's monstrous clutches. Hannah's frantic screams were now whimpers. God. He was killing her. Liberty dug her nails into his cheek and raked as deeply as she could. He snarled and with a sweep of his arm, flung her off his back. She flew into the porch railing. The air whooshed from her chest, and her vision dimmed. She squeezed her eyes shut and clenched her teeth, sucking in the cool evening air to clear her head. She couldn't pass out. Had to help Hannah.

She struggled to her feet and searched the porch, the ground, looking for something to stop the assault.

The front door opened, and her gaze flew to Antoine. With half her terrified mind, she noticed he wore a robe. They must have woken him. He held a gun. Thank God! He aimed at the vampire's back and fired.

The vampire froze for a split second, then lurched back. Hannah sank to the ground. Antoine advanced, firing round after round into the fallen vampire's chest. The vampire jerked, then went still.

"Hannah!" Liberty stumbled over and dropped to the ground on her knees. She lifted the girl's limp form into her arms. Blood poured from a wound in her neck. Trembles started in Liberty's chest, moving through her until her entire body shook.

The smell of smoldering flesh filled the air, but Liberty didn't watch the vampire disintegrate. Her focus was on Hannah. She was barely aware of the sound of a car engine. Of a slamming door. Of Eli as he vaulted onto the porch. "Liberty? Are you okay?"

"I'm—Oh God, I'm fine, but Hannah…"

"She's lost a lot of blood," Antoine said from

somewhere above Liberty's head.

Eli knelt on the other side of Hannah. Liberty faced him across the girl, her heart laden with guilt and grief. Hannah was here because of her. A sob left her throat. "She's dead, isn't she?"

Chapter 10

Liberty couldn't stop shaking, couldn't stop sobbing. Couldn't let go of the limp young girl.

Eli took hold of Liberty's arm. "You can save her." His voice was low, hoarse. His face showed tension, like he was holding himself back. Realization dawned. He was hungry. For blood. Revulsion clogged her chest.

She swallowed a lump that formed in her throat. "How?"

"Your blood. It heals."

"My blood? But how do I…?" There was already so much blood. So very much blood on Hannah's slender neck, dripping down onto her shoulders, her chest. Liberty shuddered and closed her eyes. "How can I get my blood… in her?"

"Here." This from Antoine.

Liberty opened her eyes and looked up at him. He held out a syringe.

She shuddered. The thought of plunging a needle into her skin, of watching the blood leave her veins. She choked back bile. "I can't."

Eli's gaze captured hers. "Then she'll die."

She drew in a shuddering breath. "You do it. Take my blood. I can't do that to myself."

Eli shook his head. "I might be… tempted."

Her mouth curled with distaste. She looked up at Antoine. "Can you do it? Take my blood?"

He nodded, and she held out her arm. Antoine squatted and pushed back her sleeve. He took a tourniquet and a packet of rubbing alcohol from the pocket of his robe. He tied the tourniquet around her bicep and swabbed the inside of her elbow. She couldn't help but be impressed—flabbergasted—by his readiness.

He looked up and met her gaze. "I am nothing if not prepared."

She managed a grin, then closed her eyes, unable to watch as he inserted the needle. A sting pierced her arm. She gritted her teeth, trying not to think about the blood draining from her vein.

"Done."

She opened her eyes. Red liquid filled the syringe. Antoine leaned over Hannah and brought it to her lips, then pressed the plunger. Blood trickled into her mouth.

Sickness coiled through Liberty's belly, but her worry for Hannah compelled her to watch. Color returned to the girl's cheeks. The wound on her neck healed in front of Liberty's eyes. Disbelief and relief washed through her. *It worked. It actually worked.*

Hannah's lids batted open. She rose to a sitting position and shook her head wildly from side to side. Her eyes widened in terror. "What happened? I was attacked. Oh my God. Was that a—a vampire?"

"Hannah, it's okay."

Her lip trembled, and she let out a screaming sob. "Oh God. A vampire! Oh my God."

"It's okay. Shhh."

Liberty reached out to comfort her, but Hannah shoved her hands away, stumbling to her feet. Her entire body shook, and her wails increased in volume.

Liberty stood and whirled to Eli. "Help her."

"Help her?"

"You can make her forget, right?"

The girl was backing away, close to the edge of the porch, terror making her reckless.

Eli took hold of her shoulders, stopping her backward momentum.

"Let me go!" she screamed. "Let me go. All of you, stay away from me."

Eli cupped her face in his hands. "Hannah. Look at me."

She tried to jerk away, but Eli's grip held her still. "Hannah, you're fine. Look into my eyes. You'll be fine."

The girl stilled and stared into his face.

He spoke softly, calmly. "You won't remember what happened. You came here to Liberty's house, and she took you inside. You spent the night with her. Nothing else happened."

"I spent the night with Liberty," she repeated robotically. "Nothing else happened."

He smiled. "That's right. That's a good girl. You're going to be fine."

"I'm going to be fine."

"And you will not, under any circumstances, go out alone after dark."

She nodded.

Eli dropped his hands and turned to Liberty. "Find her another shirt. Put her to bed. She won't remember any of this."

"Thanks," she whispered, wrapping her arm around Hannah's shoulder and leading her to the door. Now that her fear for Hannah had subsided, a question nagged at her. She turned back to Eli. "How did you know we were in trouble?"

"I heard your screams."

"Heard? But… you were… gone."

"Vampires have extra sensitive hearing." He winked. "So don't talk about me behind my back."

She smiled. "I can't make any promises."

****

The morning after Hannah's visit, Liberty returned the girl to her grandparents. She told them part of the truth. About Hannah sneaking out and going to bars. She didn't want to be a snitch, but maybe they'd keep a closer eye on her, and she'd be safe. Besides, half the truth was better than the whole truth. For everyone.

The night of the full moon came too soon. Liberty was so on edge, she didn't feel like eating a bite. Antoine insisted she needed sustenance, so she'd conceded and choked down a little bit of fruit and a protein shake.

Just before sundown, she shoved the pistol, a couple of magazines loaded with wooden bullets, wooden stakes, and the quiver filled with arrows into a duffle bag, then laid the bow next to the bag. After the incident with Hannah, Eli had insisted she keep weapons at the house. She hadn't argued.

The doorbell pealed. She opened it to find Ryan on the porch.

"What are you doing here?"

"I told you. I wouldn't let you go without me."

"You can't come. It's not safe."

He stepped closer. "How can I stay away? Knowing what you'll be facing?"

She opened her mouth to reply, but he bent his head, captured her mouth with his. The suddenness of the kiss… the intensity, took her by surprise. Then he was pulling back, taking it away just when she was starting to enjoy it. She put her hands on his shoulders and pressed her lips more firmly to his. A small groan spilled from him, and he tightened his arms around her, deepening the kiss.

Her stomach quivered, warmth pulsing through her blood. Her legs nearly buckled. God. He was a good kisser. Cam had never kissed her like this. Not even close.

He pulled back and placed his hand on the back of her neck, staring into her eyes. "I think I'm falling in love with you, Liberty."

Still swoony and hazy from the kiss, it took a moment for his words to sink in. Then shock rendered her speechless. Ryan was falling in love with her? Her heart hammered in her chest, and her stomach knotted. Did she love him? She cared about him. But love? If she loved him, would she have these confusing feelings about Eli?

She swallowed the dryness in her throat. "I don't know what to say."

"You don't have to say anything. I just wanted you to know. All I want is for you to give us a shot. Can you do that?"

Could she? He was kind, sexy. He made her feel safe and cherished. Yes. She smiled. She could do that. She nodded, and Ryan tilted his head forward, then his lips met hers again. He settled his hands on her hips, pressed her against his hard body. She sighed with pleasure.

"Well, what have we here?"

She jumped back at the sound of Eli's voice. Lifting a hand to her mouth, she looked up at Ryan. He winked, then turned to where Eli stood in the doorway. "Just a kiss for good luck."

Eli frowned and stepped inside. "As touching as that scene was, she needs to focus on tonight. No distractions. And you need to get home, safe inside."

Ryan shook his head. "No can do. I'm coming."

Eli's jaw tightened. "We've been over this. You can't come."

"You don't run the show, Eli. I'm coming, no matter what you say."

"Don't think so." Eli moved in a flash and elbowed Ryan in the gut. Ryan grunted and doubled over.

Liberty let out scream. "Eli! Stop it."

He ignored her, plowing his fist into Ryan's jaw. Ryan went slack and fell to the floor. Liberty dropped to her knees beside him and turned to look up at Eli. Fury made her almost unable to speak. "Are you insane? What the hell do you think you're doing?"

"Saving his ass. Make yourself useful and get me something to tie him up with."

"Screw you. You did that because you saw us kissing."

Eli snorted a laugh and gripped her arm, pulling her to her feet. He yanked her close, until their faces were only centimeters apart. "Grow up. This isn't high school, and I don't give a damn who you kiss. This is about keeping the idiot from getting himself killed. Now if you ever want to enjoy another of his swoon worthy make out sessions, I'd suggest you do what the hell I say." He released her with a small shove. She stumbled back, rubbing her arm where he'd held her. He hadn't hurt her, but his touch was too… disturbing… confusing. And in spite of her anger. He was right. Ryan had to be stopped. For his own good.

Antoine came into the foyer and looked down at Ryan, then up at Eli. "I assume there is a reasonable explanation for this."

"There is, but no time for that right now. Tie him up. Make sure he can't get free. He'll wake soon."

Antoine nodded. Eli said to Liberty, "You ready?"

She snatched her bag off the floor and followed him to his car, her lips tightened in mutinous silence. He might have had a reason for doing what he'd done, but he could have been a little gentler.

They drove into town. Eli tried to make conversation, but she refused to speak.

"I guess we are still in high school," he muttered beneath his breath.

He pulled to a stop in the parking lot of a bar called Steamy Nights. "This is a good place to start."

This was it. Was she really going through with this? Her heart plummeted to her stomach. No. She couldn't do it.

"No way. No way. No way." She didn't realize she was mumbling the words aloud until she felt Eli's touch on her forearm.

"It's going to be okay." His voice was low, soothing. "I know it's scary, but this is what you trained for."

She nodded and swiped at her eyes where tears wouldn't stop welling. "I'm okay."

"Look at me." Eli cupped her chin in his fingers and turned her to face him. "It's not too late. You don't have to do this."

"I—It's my destiny. It's what I've trained for."

"Yeah, but you can walk away. Get on the next flight out. Go back to Oklahoma and forget you ever met any of us. Forget you're a Van Helsing."

She studied him intently. "Is that what you would do?"

He compressed his lips. "We're not talking about me. This isn't your world."

She drew in a lungful of air and let it out slowly. "It is now. Let's do this."

They climbed from the car, and Eli led her to an alley alongside the bar. "You can wait here. Stay covered. They'll have weapons too. When you see one, take them down. Male or female. Adult or child."

She shook her head emphatically. "No way. I can't kill a child. That's where I draw the line."

He quirked a grin. "You'll eventually get over that. You have no idea how evil the little bastards can be."

"Eli!"

"Oh, Liberty. So naïve." He shook his head. "Here. Make sure your vest is secure." He tugged the zipper on her vest. Was it her imagination, or had his hands lingered just briefly on her breasts? She looked up into his face. He shuttered his lids over his eyes and dropped his hands, then cleared his throat. "All set. It's best to use the bow if possible. It's soundless and won't alert the others to your position. Any questions?"

"Not right now. I'll let you know if I think of any."

"You'd better ask them now."

"Why?"

He heaved out a sigh but didn't respond.

Then it hit her. No way. He wouldn't do that. Would he? "You—you're leaving me? You said you would be with me. By my side. That I wouldn't do this alone."

He lifted his hands out, palms up. "Lesson learned. You can't trust anything I say."

"I don't believe this. You asshole!"

He slowly nodded. "Not an inaccurate assessment. But this time, I have a reason for being one. I have to take care of something." He looked up at the sky. "Full moon, remember?"

She ground her teeth together. She should have known she couldn't trust him. What was his deal? He'd given her the opportunity to save herself, now he was throwing her to the wolves—or rather, vampires.

She let out a bitter laugh. "Oh yeah. I forgot. You have to turn someone. Are you turning someone who wants to be turned?"

"Would it make you feel better if I said yes?"

She thought about it. "Not really. Knowing you're forcing someone—destroying a life—will fit in with the opinion I now have of you."

His eyes narrowed, and his lips tightened. For a second, she saw a glimpse of some emotion come and go in his eyes. Then, the cocky grin was back. "Then I guess we're all set. Good luck."

He turned his back and walked away. Left her there. Alone. Scared. And completely out of her element.

Chapter 11

Liberty stashed the duffle bag behind a post in the back corner of the alley. Her hands trembled as she slid three stakes in the loops of her vest and tucked the gun in the back of her belt. She strapped the quiver to her back and slung the bow over her shoulder. Fully armed. Now what? *Now, you kill vampires.* Her chest ached with dread.

It wasn't too late to call it off. She could leave now. Get a ride back to the house. She needed to check on Ryan anyway. Eli had hit him pretty hard. She could forget all this insanity and just… walk away.

But she wouldn't. That wasn't what she'd trained for. Running away wasn't in the Van Helsing DNA. Victor was afraid for her to carry on his legacy, but it was the right thing to do. She would honor him by heeding the call of her destiny, even if it killed her.

She took a few steps and stopped. Her legs shook so violently, she wasn't sure she could go any farther. Closing her eyes, she inhaled a deep breath, then let it out slowly. She reached into her pants pocket and tightened her fingers around Ryan's coin. It warmed in her grip. Calming her. A little. Not enough. Her stomach still fluttered, and she felt like she might hurl.

Come on, Liberty. You can do this. You have to do this.

She forced one leg in front of the other until they

carried her to the mouth of the alley. With her back to the wall, she peeked out into the street.

Streetlights cast a glow along the road, but nothing moved. Loud music and laughter filtered into the night from the bar. She made her way cautiously into the street, keeping to the shadows. Most of the businesses were closed. Steamy Nights and a couple of restaurants seemed to be the only places open.

She hung around outside the bar for thirty minutes or so, then started patrolling the side streets. She covered every inch of town in just under an hour, then focused her attention on the main road. If anything was going down, it would likely happen there.

As she strolled, she looked up at the full white moon hanging low in the velvet sky. A beautiful night on a beautiful island. And she was hunting vampires. Or was she? She had no idea where to look. There didn't seem to be very many people out. Human or vampire. Maybe Eli was mistaken. Maybe even the EO's had decided to stay in tonight. Maybe—

Footsteps sounded behind her, and she whirled, reaching instinctively for the bow. A vampire stalked toward her, fangs glistening in the lights of the streetlamps. She fumbled in the quiver, but before her fingers could grip an arrow, the vampire was on her. He grabbed the back of her head and tilted it back. His fangs hovered above her neck, poised to strike. She knew what might happen to him if he bit her. She had no idea what it might do to her. And she didn't want to find out.

"I'm a Van Helsing," she shouted.

He froze, then released her and lurched back. His red eyes narrowed, as if considering the truth of her claim. A low growl emitted from his throat. He reached into the pocket of his jacket. She drew a stake from her vest. No time to use the bow.

He withdrew his hand, and moonlight glinted on silver metal. *Shit*. He had a gun.

He aimed, and she dove to the ground, the stake skittering out of her hand, clattering on the asphalt. A shot rang out, and a burning, stinging pain ripped through her forearm. She reached behind her and pulled her own gun, aiming with both hands, just as he was aiming a second time. She fired off three shots, and he dropped.

She waited for her heartbeat to slow and her breath to ease, then warily made her way to his side. She had to insure that the wooden bullets hit their target—his heart. If not, she would have to shoot him again. She wasn't sure she could. Not again.

But there was no need. Two of the three bullets had hit the mark dead center. She gritted her teeth in a humorless smile. Eli would be impressed.

She came to her feet and looked down at her injury. The bullet had only nicked her, but it was enough to draw blood. The fluid seeped down her arm and onto her hand, painting bright red drops on the street.

"Oh God," she gasped. Her eyes clouded over. Queasiness crawled from her chest to her throat. She clenched her teeth and sucked in air. She had to treat it. Had to wrap it. She couldn't continue to bleed. She would pass out, then she would be screwed.

She glanced down at the vampire. She had to move quickly, in a matter of seconds, it would be too late. She knelt beside the body and used a stake to rip a hole in his shirt, then tugged until a strip of fabric tore free. She wrapped it around her arm and tucked the ends beneath her sleeve to hold it in place. Not the best bandage job in the world, but it should stop the bleeding. Nothing she could do about the blood already on her skin. She would have to ignore it if she wanted to stay conscious. She'd no more than stepped back than the body burst into flames, then sizzled away to ashes.

She gathered the stake and her bow and seated them back in place. Weakness assailed her limbs. She should have eaten more. Antoine was right. She needed sustenance. She watched the dust of the vampire scatter in the night breeze. Why didn't it bother her more that she'd taken a life? Was it because he was a vampire—a killer? Or was it her hunter instincts? Maybe tomorrow, she would fall apart. But now, she only felt a renewed energy—a sense of satisfaction.

She headed back up the street, now almost hoping she would have an opportunity to take out another vampire. Although she knew it wasn't right, it was how she felt. What was wrong with her? She shouldn't be so calm.

A man and woman with their arms linked together weaved out the door of Steamy Nights. The man glanced at her, at the weapons strapped to her body, and his eyes rounded. He ducked his head and hurried the woman down the sidewalk.

She walked up and down the street. Nearly two hours had passed since her encounter with the vampire. Was that it? The town was so still… so silent. The adrenaline rush had abated, and while she still felt no remorse, her enthusiasm had waned. She should just go home. Eli hadn't said anything about picking her up, and she hadn't asked. She could walk, although it was quite a distance.

She'd almost reached the alley, ready to retrieve the duffle bag and head back when she glanced across the street. A man had a woman pressed against the door of a closed dress shop. Liberty ambled closer. The woman's dark hair was tangled around her face. Her eyes were wide with—fear? Pain? Bliss?—but she didn't make a sound. The vampire was oblivious to Liberty's presence as he fed from his victim's neck.

Liberty pulled out an arrow, loaded it, and aimed. She released, and the arrow pierced the vampire's lower back. The vampire spasmed and flailed his hand behind him. His fingers latched on to the arrow and tugged. Liberty stalked over to him, loading another arrow on the move, then quickly released the string. The wooden barb landed in the center of his chest. His movements stilled, and he tumbled to the sidewalk.

A moan drew her attention to the woman. She slid down the side of the building to the ground, eyes closed. Liberty ran to her and gently lifted her chin. She was about Liberty's age. Pretty, with flawless skin. Skin that was now pale, lifeless. Her throat was nearly torn open from the viciousness of the vampire's assault. Liberty put her fingers to the woman's wrist. Barely a pulse. The girl was going to die if Liberty didn't do something.

Your blood heals...

Liberty looked down at her injured arm, horrified by the thought. But she had to do what she could to save the girl.

Liberty cradled the woman's head in her lap and shoved her forearm to the victim's mouth. Most of the blood had dried, but surely it would still work. She wasn't quite willing to remove the cloth and feed her fresh blood—unless she had to.

With another moan, the woman tasted the blood Liberty offered. Liberty cringed, waiting to see if it worked—if the neck wound would heal. If the girl would live.

She continued to greedily suck the blood. Something wasn't right. She was enjoying the blood too much…

Her eyes popped open. Red eyes…

Oh God. I saved a vampire.

The woman snatched a stake from Liberty's vest and rose to her feet. Liberty dropped her hold and crab walked backward. The woman advanced, holding the stake in the air.

Liberty retreated, reaching for the gun on her belt. The vampire came to a standstill and looked at the stake in her hand. She frowned as if in bewilderment, then lifted the stake and raked the pointed end along her own arm. Liberty let out a scream as the woman jabbed the sharp wood into her stomach. A guttural cry tore from her lips, yet she still plunged the stake into her flesh over and over.

Liberty couldn't react. Couldn't move. She watched in horrified silence as blood gushed from the wounds the woman continued to inflict. Self mutilating. Because Liberty had fed her Van Helsing blood. Sickened and guilty, Liberty tried to turn away, but she couldn't. With one last pain-filled cry, the vampire drove the stake into her heart. She quivered for several agonizing seconds, then crumpled into a heap.

Oh God, oh God, oh God.

Liberty tamped back the bile that rose to her throat and pushed wearily to her feet. She'd had enough for one night. Maybe she wasn't meant to be a hunter after all.

Unable to take her eyes off the bloody female, unable to turn from the sight as the poor girl became a smoldering pile of dust, she backed slowly away. And came up against a hard figure. She spun. A man reached out to steady her, but she evaded his grip. He was dark-haired, muscular, and most likely, a vampire.

He lowered his head and cocked it from side to side like a parakeet. "My, my. You *are* a tasty treat." A lopsided grin caused a dimple to appear at the right side of his mouth. "You must be Liberty. I've heard so much about you."

"Who are you?" She continued to put distance between them.

"I'm Trey. Trey Logan. Pleased to meet you, Liberty." He drew her name out slowly, rolling it around on his tongue as if he were sampling a wine. "Unusual name—Liberty, as in freedom. Kind of ironic, since you're about to lose yours."

She fumbled for her gun, and he lifted a finger and waved it in front of his face, tut-tutting her as if she were a naughty child.

"We don't need weapons. This is just a friendly chat." He looked her up and down. "I can see why Rupert is so intrigued by you. A gorgeous, young *female* Van Helsing. Why wouldn't he be? As a matter of fact, I'd like to keep you for my own."

"Keep me?" She tried to make her laugh sound derisive, but it came out sounding like a cry for help. "I'm not an object."

"No? Are you sure about that?"

He moved a few steps closer. She stood her ground, debating whether to try for the gun after all. He wasn't exactly threatening, but she didn't feel exactly safe, either.

He closed his eyes and inhaled deeply. "Ah, you smell delicious. Like Nirvana." His eyes popped open, and he grinned. "Not Nirvana—the rock band. The heavenly, blissful one." He licked his lips and let out a regretful sigh. "It's true what they say, you know. The things we desire most are those that are bad for us. Your blood is so… tempting. I don't just want to *drink* it, I want to bathe in it."

She shuddered at the image. "Oh, is that all you want? My blood?" She shoved her arm out and offered her wrist. "Here. Have some."

He threw his head back and bellowed a laugh. "Ah, Liberty. You are delightful."

He reached for her, and she turned to run. A shot rang out, and she looked back over her shoulder.

Trey jerked, his face scrunching in pain. He squinted at her, and his mouth spread into a smile that was more a flinch. "Missed the heart, but that's my cue. Until we meet again… Liberty." In one quick movement, he was gone. She wasn't sure if he'd disappeared or if he'd moved so fast, he just *seemed* to disappear.

Eli stood six feet away. He shoved a gun into the back of his waistband.

She ran to him. He held out his arms and drew her close, soothing a hand over her back. "It's okay," he murmured. "I've got you. It's okay."

His arms were too warm, being in them felt too… right. When her trembling subsided, she pulled away.

He lifted his hand and wiped her tears away with his thumb. "So," he said softly. "How was your first hunt?"

She thought of the kill… then of the vampire she'd inadvertently caused to commit hara-kiri.

A shaky laugh escaped. "Interesting. Scary." She stepped back. "What about you? Did you turn someone?"

He nodded, his jaw tight. His gaze moved down to her arm, and he frowned. "You're hurt."

She looked down at her arm. Blood leaked from under the wrapping. The world tilted, and she closed her eyes. "Oh God. I'm going to be sick. *Blood.* I can't handle…" The strength left her legs. "I need to sit down."

He took hold of her uninjured arm. "You have got to be kidding me. You're afraid of blood?" He scowled. "You'd think that's a piece of info you might have shared. That's kind of a detriment to a vampire hunter."

"Just cover it up, please."

He led her to the sidewalk in front of Steamy Nights and eased her down so she was leaning her back against the building beneath a window. Light shone down on them, and music spilled out from the club.

He gently unwrapped the cloth and reached beneath his shirt to tear a strip of material off the wife beater he wore underneath. He swiped at the dried blood with the cloth he'd removed. "What did I do to be saddled with you?"

The wooziness was subsiding, and she smiled. "I guess you shouldn't be such a stud at training hunters."

He laughed. "I guess not." He tossed the bloody strip of material away and wrapped the fresh cloth over her injury. "Let's hope the vampire this shirt belonged to practiced good hygiene. The last thing you need is an infected wound."

"No kidd—" She halted and narrowed her eyes at him. "How did you know where I got this?"

"What?" He dropped his gaze, busying himself with tying the strip of material around her wound.

"How did you know I took the cloth from a vampire's shirt?"

He shrugged. "Lucky guess?"

She made a buzzer noise. "Wrong answer. You were watching me. Making sure I was okay."

"No I wasn't. I had my own bullshit to deal with."

A rush of affection welled in her chest. "But you did it, then came back so you could watch over me."

"Yeah, right. You must have lost too much blood. You're hallucinating."

"You were worried. Why didn't you let me know you were around? I would have been a lot less scared."

He compressed his lips and took his time answering. "You needed to find out what you were capable of. If you knew I was around, you might have depended on me instead of on yourself."

So, he'd helped her by not helping her. She grinned. "That's so… sweet."

He grunted. "I'm anything but sweet. Let's just drop it, okay?"

"Okay. Whatever." She drew in a deep, cleansing breath, the cool air easing her sickness. It also helped that Eli had cleaned the blood off and re-wrapped her wound. "You'd think my own blood could heal me. It heals others."

"You'd think. But it doesn't." He looked up at her, his eyes glittering with a smile. "You did well. You're much tougher, much braver than I thought."

She snorted a laugh. "So, you thought I would wimp out?"

"It crossed my mind. But you didn't." He brushed a

strand of hair back from her face and let his fingers linger on her cheek. "Ryan's a good dude. You should have babies with him and forget all this craziness."

He was close... too close. Her pulse jumped, her throat so dry it made a clicking sound when she swallowed. "Is that what you want me to do?"

He dropped his hand from her face and studied her, jaw clenched.

Running footsteps pounded on the asphalt. "You son of a bitch."

Liberty looked behind Eli to where Ryan was advancing, his fists clenched at his sides. Eli stood and glanced over one shoulder, then the other, then back at Ryan with a mocking smile. "Who, me?"

"You could have gotten her killed, you bloody drongo."

"Don't go berko, mate." Eli's voice held amusement as he mocked Ryan's accent. "You're the one who insisted I train her to be a hunter."

Ryan had reached him now, and he drew back his fist and plowed it into Eli's mouth. Eli's head jerked back, but he didn't go down.

Breathing heavily, Ryan panted, "You didn't have to shut me out. I should have been here."

Liberty gasped and struggled to her feet. "Ryan, stop!"

Eli wiped the back of his hand over his mouth and gripped Ryan's throat, lifting him off the ground. Ryan clutched at Eli's hands and gasped for air, his face red, the veins sticking out like worms beneath his skin.

"Eli!" Liberty grabbed hold of Eli's arm. "Let him go."

Eli ignored her. "You seem to be forgetting the

pecking order around here." His voice was low, deadly. "Don't test me."

Eli tossed him away. Ryan flew back and landed hard on the concrete.

Liberty rushed to his side. "Are you okay?"

"I'm fine." He pushed to his feet, rubbing his throat as he glared at Eli. "Does she know why I wanted you to train her? Why *you* were the best one for the job?"

Eli looked at Liberty, an unreadable expression in his silver eyes. He brought his gaze back to Ryan without speaking.

"She doesn't know, does she?" Ryan taunted.

"Know what?" Liberty looked from Ryan to Eli. "Know what?" she gritted through clenched teeth.

"Tell her, Eli. Tell her the reason you know so much about the EO's is because you were once one yourself."

Eli let out a heavy breath and closed his eyes.

Liberty's heart plummeted to her stomach. "Is that true?"

Eli was once a vicious, murdering vampire, just like the ones she'd been fighting tonight? She stared at him, wanting him to deny the accusation. Knowing in her soul he wouldn't.

"It's true," Ryan said. "Less than a year ago, he was just like them. I'm not so sure there isn't some part of him that still is."

Liberty looked at Eli, her brows raised in question.

He shrugged. "It's true. I was one of them."

"What… why didn't you tell me?"

He stepped closer and captured her gaze with his. "Because, I don't owe you anything. Not an explanation. Not the truth. Nothing."

"I—I trusted you."

He shrugged. "I warned you about that. About trusting too easily. You didn't listen. Maybe from now on, you'll be more cautious."

She swallowed a knot of pain, not responding.

He gave a little salute, then turned and stalked away.

Liberty blinked back tears and brought her attention back to Ryan. "Are you okay? Did he hurt you?" *Like he hurt me?*

"He didn't hurt me. I'm fine. How about you? Are you okay?"

She nodded. "I'm great now that you're here."

"I'm sorry I put you in danger. I couldn't live with myself if anything happened to you."

"You didn't put me in danger. I did that myself. I don't regret it."

He cupped her face in both his hands and pressed a kiss on her forehead. "Let's get you home, love."

"Trust me. I'm more than ready. I hope you drove. I don't think I could walk another step."

He laughed and looped his arm over her shoulder. "Yes. I drove. The rest of the night, all you have to worry about is being pampered."

Being pampered sounded good. She let him lead her to the parking lot and to his car. For now, she needed peace, sleep, and to stop thinking about Eli. Ryan was all she needed, all she wanted.

For now.

An Excerpt from *Liberty Divided*, Book 2 in the Isle of Fangs Series…

Prologue

Sang Croc Island
French Polynesia

The night breeze blowing in from the ocean brought with it the intoxicating aromas of suntan oil and blood. Although there weren't a lot of humans on the beach now that dusk had fallen, the heady scent of the rich, red fluid was strong enough that the vampire could still smell it just beneath the surface of their flesh. He drew in a breath and slowly exhaled. *Delicious.*

The sliver of moon drifted in the black sky and shone on the white sand, providing enough light so that, even if he weren't a vampire, he could still see clearly.

He strolled along the beach, blending in with the handful of human tourists hanging about. He'd been itching for the sun to go down, had barely slept all day. He was hungry. Jonesing for a feed. Mostly, though, he was anxious to put the next phase of his plan in motion. Slow and steady. Wasn't that how the tortoise had won the race?

He strode across the soft sand, looking out at the glassy surface of the ocean—a sight he would never see the way it was meant to be seen, in sunlight. The cruel irony of being a vampire on a tropical island wasn't lost on him.

Ah well, while he was unable to enjoy the daytime,

fortunately, beautiful, tasty women were always out in abundance, even after darkness fell.

Evidence of his prediction came when he spotted two girls in barely-there bikinis at the edge of the ocean. They kicked water on one another, giggling and squealing in oblivious delight.

Girls. They were the easiest.

They passed a bottle of Lambrusco back and forth, chugging straight from the neck. He grinned. How fitting. In a matter of moments, *he* would be chugging straight from the neck.

He approached silently, not speaking until he was within a foot of where they frolicked. "Ladies? Enjoying yourselves?"

They turned startled eyes on him. The expression on the tall brunette's face became a flirty smile. The shorter of the two still looked wary.

"Tons," the brunette said. She held out the bottle. "Want a sip?"

His lips spread into a grin. "More than you can imagine."

She laughed and released the Lambrusco into his grip. He put it to his mouth and drank. The wine was a cheap, sweet red. The taste couldn't compare to the sweet red of the blood flowing through the girls' veins. Veins he would tap into shortly.

"Skyler, we'd better be heading back to the hotel," Miss Blond, Short, and Skeptical said to her friend.

He moved closer to the blonde and walked into the ocean, ignoring the unpleasant feeling of water-soaked shoes. He stared down, letting his eyes capture hers. "Why is that? The party's only just begun."

She swallowed audibly, and the pulse in her neck

jumped. Excitement bloomed in his chest. He hadn't been sure which one would die, but now he knew. This one had spunk. She would not only taste delicious, conquering her would be more exciting.

She started to look away, but he gripped her chin in his fingers. "What's your name?" he asked softly.

"Mine's Skyler," her friend said from behind him, as if he hadn't just heard the blonde call her by name. "She can go back to the hotel if she wants and—"

"Silence!" He whirled on the brunette. She blinked at him in hurt confusion. Sensitive little thing. For God's sake. It wasn't like he said her bikini made her look fat.

Still holding the blonde's chin, he focused on the brunette's eyes. "Look at me and listen carefully." He kept his voice low, commanding. "Stand there quietly and don't move. Don't make a sound until I tell you it's okay. Understand?"

"Hey," her blond friend said. "You can't tell her what to do."

He let out a frustrated breath. Mesmerizing two chicks at once was not an easy feat.

He turned back to the blonde and made sure they were eye to eye. Made sure he had her complete attention. "You will also be quiet. Do exactly as I say. Understand?"

A frown marred her brows, but she gave a quick, jerky nod. Barely under. Good. He didn't want her too docile when the time came.

Back to the brunette, he said, "No matter what happens, no matter what you see, you won't make a peep. You won't move. Got it?"

She nodded and immediately quieted. The only sounds were those of crashing waves and distant conversations of other humans.

"Your name?" he demanded again.

"Patrice," she finally muttered.

"Well, Patrice, because you're so enticing, so remarkable, you will have to be sacrificed. But take solace in the fact that your friend will be spared."

She blinked rapidly. Her mouth dropped open, and little mewling sounds came out. "What? I… you're going to…?"

He released her chin and gripped a handful of hair at the back of her head. "Not a sound, I said." She fell silent, and he reveled in the terror-filled eyes. So easy.

He yanked her to him and tugged her head back. With a growl, he protracted his fangs and drove them deep into her flesh.

Hot sweet blood with just a hint of wine flowed into his mouth. He nearly moaned in satisfaction. The feeding was good… great, but being another step closer to exacting revenge… well, that was about as good as it got.

She struggled silently, clawing at his shoulders, trying to shove him away. Nice. He liked a little fight. But the fight soon fled. Her body went limp. The flow of blood slowed. Her heart no longer pumped it to him. He released her, and her body hit the water with a splash.

He turned back to her friend, wiping his mouth with the back of his hand. Silent tears coursed down her cheeks. Her body trembled violently, but she remained silent, standing where he'd left her.

He ignored the flicker of sympathy crowding its way into his soul. He was a vampire, after all. It was in his nature to feed… to kill. No room for a conscience. No room for weakness.

He stalked to the brunette and grabbed her

shoulders, looking down into her eyes. "Listen carefully," he said. "I want you to wait ten minutes, then run up the beach, screaming. Report this to the police. You understand?"

She nodded.

"Good. And this is what you'll tell them…"

A word about the author…

Alicia Dean lives in Edmond, Oklahoma and is the mother of three grown children. Alicia loves creating spine-chilling stories that keep readers on the edge of their seats. She's a huge Elvis Presley fan, and loves MLB and the NFL. If you look closely, you'll see a reference to one or all three in pretty much everything she writes. If she could, she would divide all her time between writing, watching her favorite television shows-such as Dexter, Vampire Diaries, Justified, and True Blood-and reading her favorite authors… Stephen King, Dennis Lehane, Michael Connelly, Lee Child, and Lisa Gardner to name a few.

Please follow Alicia on Twitter: @Alicia_Dean_ and visit her website: AliciaDean.com, or feel free to drop her a line at: AliciaMDean@aol.com.